Likely Stories

By Mick Stern

D1714355

This book and my heart
are both dedicated to Naomi

Book cover design and all artwork by Mick Stern

Without Anesthesia

Why did she leave me? Where did she go? They said her heart was encrypted and password-protected. She was my No-Annual-Fee, two-drink-minimum downfall. Sometimes she was a walk in the park, sometimes a waltz on a slippery floor, but to me she was always Anesthesia Chevynova, daughter of her bloody tribe. I met her at a wedding in Lower Nowhere. The family passed around a bottle of grape-mango bubbly to toast the beaming couple. After several minutes of beaming, the couple vanished completely, leaving a faint smudge in the air. They materialized at a reception in a roof garden. Guests were arriving molecule by molecule.

I sensed that somebody alluring was emerging by the buffet. I decided to play it cool, keep it light. As soon as she was fully opaque I said, "I hope you are single? I need you so badly!"

"Your name, please, " she said sharply.

"I come from the illustrious family of Lancaster, which over time became Lackluster."

Anesthesia suddenly turned pale, and fell upon a couch so dramatically that her bodice almost ripped.

She said, "Alas, what misery, to experience a love that is doomed forever by the first words of the beloved!"

"You mean you loved me the moment you saw me?"

"No, the moment I heard your name! You see, I am a gypsy and forbidden to marry outside my tribe. It is the aura of the forbidden that I find irresistible. That aside, you're about a B minus if the light is dim and flattering."

Her remarks didn't hurt my pride. They annihilated it.

We took a ride to the river to see the moon over oily water. But she was nervous, didn't want to stay out too long, for fear that her parents would sell the apartment and leave town without her. And her deepest fears were realized. When we stepped out of the cab, her parents' house was dark.

I chattered away, trying to divert her.

"How do you like that? Did they even leave a note? Looks like they took everything with them. Oh my God, you poor thing, it must be a joke, right, a joke?"

"Shut up," she said.

"And now they're gone—who knows where."

Anesthesia slid to the floor. "They went nowhere and took the dining room with them. That's how they are."

"But why? I don't understand it."

"Because of you." She shrugged. "They knew about us from the start. They have spies everywhere." Anesthesia cuddled close to me. "I'm afraid," she said.

I took her hand and we walked down insignificant streets toward a cheese Danish dawn. A car was following us—a gypsy cab, I saw to my dismay.

The horn beeped and the driver shouted, "Anesthesia, you must come with me!"

She shouted back, "Who's paying you to imitate a human being, you dumb gorilla?"

"Your parents, who else?" He pointed at me. "Get rid of the doofus. You're ruining the family name!"

"Don't tell me what to do with my doofus. Who the hell are you, anyway?" said Anesthesia.

"I am Tomatito Gold Molars, at your service. Don't you know that since you left, your mother cries in the dark and your grandmother has fleas. I won't even tell you about your father."

"But they left me behind."

"You should have stayed in the dining room."

"Tomatito, what would it cost to convince you that you never saw me?"

The driver said, "Are you asking me to lie?"

"No, I'm paying you to lie."

He shrugged. "I guess a couple of Ben Franks would be enough to cause a convenient memory lapse." He laughed until he choked.

A few weeks later, we moved into an apartment near the Grand Concourse in the Bronx. Our lives fell into a pleasant routine. Anesthesia went to work, I stayed home. She made dinner, I ate it. She cleaned up the apartment, I messed it up, then she cleaned it again. I didn't mind this arrangement at all. But she did. "Why don't you get a friggin job?" she would say. Often.

One night when we were lying in bed she sat up suddenly. Annoyed, I said, "You just ruined a perfectly good arrangement of naked limbs! Let's see—your thigh was resting on my…"

She interrupted me. "Get a job now! No more procrastinating. Do you understand?"

I smelled gypsy blood boiling. Though it was 3 a.m., I got dressed and wandered out into the street. You don't find a lot of job offers at that hour. A ragamuffin boy, maybe ten years old, ran after me. "Hey mister, you got any candy you don't plan on eatin'?"

"As a matter of fact, I do. Tell you what. Do what I say and I'll give you all the candy you can stuff into your greedy little mouth."

"Oh goody!"

I pushed the skinny little tyke head first into the ventilation system of the Jewelers Exchange Building and instructed him to wiggle his way to the nearest display case. He came back with a magnificent diamond. I patted him on the head and told him to meet me in front of the candy store when it opened. He's probably still there waiting for me.

When I got home, Anesthesia almost barked at me. "Whaddaya got?" "How do you know I got something?" I said coyly, turning the diamond around.

I could see she was gob-smacked by its dazzle. "Give me that diamond," she said.

"I don't think so. I'm planning to mount it on a gold ring and wear it. Maybe I'll sell it and buy a pink and green sports car."

"My father and brothers are just looking for an excuse to bury you and throw away the key."

Shit! I had completely forgotten about them. I gave her the diamond. "Thanks. Are you going to find a real job? You can't live on rare diamonds."

"After intense meditation and psychoanalysis, I have discovered the Real Me, and he's unemployed."

"Have it your way, then," she said. She always said that when she had absolutely no intention of letting me have it my way. Without another word, she walked out the door. I followed her until an ungrammatical man stepped in front of me, spat on the ground and said, "Let go her, my friend. Better not be thinking about her no more."

"What do you know about her?" I said.

"Anesthesia and me gone to school together. I know this girl like my grandmother knows the attic. Forget about it, mister."

"Oh, don't worry," I said. "I have no intention of remembering even the slightest moment. I shall retain no images, no words, not even the video she made for me. Especially not that." I sniffled and blew my nose on his sleeve. He didn't seem to mind. He said, "Come, I buy for you some drinking."

He took me to a bar where a monkey danced to the rhythm of a honky-tonk piano. In between dances the monkey collected money from the crowd and spent it all on alcohol. The piano player told us that he was trying to save up enough money to buy a sober monkey. He and his monkey made an odd couple. All couples are odd. One fool marries another fool for no good reasons. Who is that going to help except Ikea?

The last moments of the evening were slipping way. I could already hear the rumble of day jobs, skyscrapers creaking in their foundations, water sloshing in the harbor.

All at once, something snapped in me. I rushed into the street not knowing where I was going or why. The next few years are a blur. I think I got a degree in Business Education.

But I'm still lost. Lost without the love of my gypsy dancer, the beautiful but encrypted Anesthesia Chevynova, daughter of her bloody tribe.

Mick

Get Out of Town

I went downtown to find Vagrant. When I got to the East Village my attention was caught by a bookstore that specialized in Wicca and the occult. Out of sheer curiosity I pushed open the door. It was hot and stuffy and the books were stacked up in precarious piles. Whoever owned this hole must have made a pact with the devil in order to stay in business. When I stepped outside, I saw Vagrant across the street.

"Hey, Vagrant!"

Vagrant crossed the street to shake hands and trade high fives. But I didn't take his long-lost-buddy enthusiasm seriously. He spent his days wandering around the East Village looking for something to do. An old and very small dog waddled alongside him. He tugged on the leash to persuade the reluctant animal to climb over a high curb.

"What's happening?" he said. "Been a while. You moved out of, where were you at? Was it Fifth Street and Avenue A?"

"I moved a year and a half ago. I live in Chelsea now."

The dog finally made it onto the sidewalk and began to lead Vagrant down the street. He said, "So you live uptown. You must meet a lot of rich chicks."

"I wish."

"You still living with your mother?"

"Yeah, but not for long. Don't tell her. She's gonna shit a brick when she hears I'm moving out."

As far as I knew, his mother had tried everything she could think of to get Vagrant to move out and on his own.

"Your dog looks a little pooped."

"He's just old."

"What's his name?"

He blushed slightly. "It's either Jeff or Kenny. I haven't made up my mind yet."

I leaned over and patted Jeff or Kenny on the head. The dog's tongue unrolled and he began to pant.

"What have you been up to?" I asked.

"The usual. You?"

This was my opening to explain that I'd been looking for him. But I couldn't quite bring myself to do it, not yet. Instead, I just shrugged. "Too much to get into. And I'd probably forget half of it. I should write it down."

"I wouldn't read it anyway," Vagrant said. "Other people bore me almost as much as I bore me" He was suddenly impatient. "Shit, it's past four already."

"Wait! I have to talk to you."

"What about?"

"I…I have to explain it."

"I hate explanations. They just confuse me."

Our stroll had brought us near a Ukrainian diner, one of the cheapest and most popular restaurants in the neighborhood. I gestured to the door. "Lunch is on me."

"I don't know."

"Come on, I really have to talk to you."

"OK. I guess."

Vagrant fumbled with Jeff or Kenny's leash and tied it to a parking meter. When Jeff or Kenny began to understand that he was going to be left out on the street alone, he barked with surprising vigor and pulled so hard at the leash he almost stood up on his hind legs. Vagrant ordered him to sit and be quiet. The dog barked. His master shouted. I finally grabbed Vagrant's arm and pulled him away.

Inside the restaurant, the warm air fogged my glasses. Vagrant said, "I heard that if you want to keep your glasses from fogging when you go indoors, you have to walk in backwards."

I bit my tongue, but didn't say a thing.

"I just heard it somewhere," he said, shrugging. "I don't wear glasses."

Everybody in the diner, regardless of gender or national origin, was dressed entirely in black and smoked cigarettes with attitude, as if posing for an album cover. The only person who didn't belong was Vagrant, and he had actually been born and raised in this neighborhood. He wore old jeans, a green and beige jacket with zippered front pockets, and white running shoes with tiny blinking LED lights. His hair was cut conservatively and combed back.

We slid into a booth, fiddled with plastic menus, and ordered.

I still didn't want to say what I had to say. "So why are you moving? What's up with that?" I asked.

"Oh that," said Vagrant. "I had this shitty job as a clerk in an art supply store. One day this woman comes in, buys something, and leaves her credit card on the counter. I grabbed the card and took off. There are all these electronics shops around Canal and Broadway run by foreigners. They'll take any card that works. The card was in the name of Sandra Liu and they were like, 'What can we do for you today, Sandra?' I charged $1,100 worth of car stereos. Car stereos always sell."

"Hey, man, this Sandra Liu chick is going find out her card is missing sooner or later."

"That's OK. Everybody knows I took it, but they can't prove anything. The credit card company, it's petty cash for them. The only one who came after me was Sandra Liu. She got my phone number somehow and called up my mom. My mom hung up on her. My mom hangs up on everybody. I don't know why she even owns a phone. Anyway, she got a bug up her ass and went snooping in my room and found the car stereos. Look, if you want one, I could give you a really great deal, you know?"

"I don't have a car."

The waiter put down two plates of cheese pierogis, sour cream in little bowls and two cups of coffee. Vagrant leaned forward and said, in a confidential tone of voice, "You can buy one or two from me and sell them uptown for double the price."

"I doubt it. Car stereos get ripped off so much that used ones cost, like, next to nothing."

"These are new car stereos. Brand new, in the original fuckin' box!" I tried a pierogi. Soft. Slightly sweet.

"Hey," Vagrant said, through a mouth full of cheese. "So what did you want to talk to me about? I ain't got all day." But he did have all day. That was the basis of our friendship or whatever it was. When I moved to New York City, Vagrant was one of the first people I met. I hung out with Vagrant almost every day after school. He was my indigenous guide to downtown Manhattan, and all he asked in return was a slice of pizza with pepperoni and a Bud Light. When I moved uptown, that was the end of our association. Or so I thought until an NYPD detective walked in my classroom last week, flashing his badge. My first thought was that he was looking for one of my students.

The detective just wanted to ask me some questions. I was not in trouble, he said. I was not the subject of the investigation. Whatever I did say would remain anonymous. I didn't believe that for a moment. I had to cooperate. We were both civil servants.

The guy wanted me to tell him everything I knew about Vagrant. He showed me a folder with some grainy photos of me and Vagrant hanging out in Tomkins Square. He repeated, in a soothing voice, that I was not in trouble, that all he wanted was information. The detective believed that Vagrant was a major downtown heroin dealer. When I tried to object to this ludicrous idea, he called me naïve and changed the subject. He said that the city was planning a crackdown on drug crime citywide, spearheaded by the NYPD, with backup from state and federal agencies. He put the photos back in their folders with a sour look on his face that made it clear that I had let him down.

Now, less than two hours later I was face to face with Vagrant.

I cleared my throat. "I have inside information that there's going to be a huge bust in the East Village. A clean sweep. They're going to make the neighborhood safe for yoga classes and boutique shopping. You know, what they did to Soho."

"Yeah? This place could sure use a change," said Vagrant as he emptied six packets of sugar into his coffee.

I tried to avoid his eyes. "This is not about a few arrests. This is going to be a fuckin' invasion." Vagrant, I don't know how to say this, but...you have to leave town."

"What the fuck are you talking about? I ain't done nothing wrong!"

"Look, Vague, let's get real. You've been a runner for a long time now."

"Only part time, when I needed money."

"That won't stand up in court."

"But I didn't do nothing!" He jumped up, rolled up his sleeve and showed a smooth, clean inner elbow. "Does that look like a junkie's arm? Huh? Huh? All I get is a free snort now and then."

"OK, OK, sit down, sit down. Now, are you absolutely sure you only sold to people you know and trusted?"

"Sure I'm sure...I hope."

"Hope isn't good enough. You gotta get out of harm's way. If you stay, they'll collar you. No doubt about it."

"How do you know? Who told you this shit? Where did you hear this evil shit?"

"A guy I know."

"You expect me to leave town because some guy who doesn't even have a name says so?"

"No, it's not a guy without a name...it was a cop." I cringed for a moment.

Vagrant said, "Why would a cop tell you... Wait a minute, did you get busted ? Now I get it! You got fuckin' busted, and you dimed on me."

"No, man, it's not like that. The cops already had your name."

"But they got more information. From you."

"Look, they're not going to chase you. You're not one of America's Ten Most Wanted or anything."

"I can't leave my mom alone."

"Just lie low in Boston or Miami for a while. You can come back eventually."

"Boston is too cold and Miami's too hot," he said. As if he'd been to either of those places.

"I should have brought some fuckin' travel brochures. I didn't know it would be so hard to convince you to stay out of jail."

"Why are you so concerned about me all of a sudden?" It was a good question. I couldn't answer it. He started putting on his coat.

"Vagrant, just leave town!"

"That is so fucked up! What am I supposed to do, walk to Florida? I have like eighteen dollars."

"I'll pay for your bus fare!"

"And when I get off the fuckin' bus, then what? You gonna pay for a hotel? I have a better idea. You should leave town. Right now, because I don't even want to fuckin' look at you anymore." He stomped out of the restaurant.

What could I say? The narcotics detectives didn't know that Anthony Zelinski aka Vagrant, spent most of his waking hours in the street because his mother didn't want him underfoot. They didn't realize that he knew all the local drug dealers because he had grown up with them on the Lower East Side. The investigators had assigned all kinds of motives to him. He didn't have any. I put on my coat and paid the check. The cash register was so old that a bell clanged when the drawer popped open.

When I stepped outside, the first thing I saw was Vagrant standing in the middle of the street shouting. "Jeff! Jeff! Kenny! Kenny!"

"What happened?" I said. "The dog slipped his leash while I was inside talking to you." The word rang with accusation.

"I'll help you find him."

He began to cry. "No, you won't, you slimy motherfucker! Get the hell out of here or I'll fuck you up!" He came at me with his fists. He was serious. I turned and ran like hell. He chased me for half a block, then abruptly turned around as if I had vanished.

Come September, I'd be standing in front of a class of twelve-year-olds. Vagrant would be in Riker's Island.

I put my hands on my thighs and bent over, breathing heavily. I kept an eye on him, but he seemed to have forgotten me. He turned and turned in every direction yelling, "Jeff! Kenny! Jeff! Kenny!"

The Autumn of the Professor

Professor Popovich didn't plan his lectures. He preferred to extemporize.

On occasion, if his mood was expansive and the topic engaged him, his lecture would become more and more fluent until he no longer had to look for words and sentences; the sentences came to him. In this near-mystic state of mind, he could lucidly articulate one idea after another without the slightest effort; it felt like the gods of wisdom were huffing and puffing on the glowing embers of his inspiration.

Then Arthur Dudley raised his hand.

Arthur Dudley sat in the back of the class, usually unshaven, always dressed in a baseball cap and sweats like an athlete in training, except that he was fat and moved cumbersomely. He had large brown sad-dog eyes that became even sadder whenever he entered the classroom. He took a seat in the last row and spent the period rolling his eyes, as if he found Popovich completely preposterous, uncannily reflecting the opinion of him that the professor was rapidly forming.

One Tuesday in September, Popovich took verbal flight on a subject dear to his heart—his dissertation topic, in fact, which he had been working on for quite a few years. His notion was that democracy was a successful political system mainly because it provided a mechanism for the orderly transferal of power. Dictatorships were inherently unstable, and therefore destructive, because they did not provide other factions within society with any legitimate access to power. Thus thwarted, these factions had no option but outright rebellion, to which the dictator could only respond with further oppression, and the implications of this were crucially important for…Popovich could no longer ignore the waving hand in the back. "Yes, Mr. Dudley?"

"Isn't the whole idea of democracy to represent the people?" he asked.

"That's the conventional wisdom," Popovich replied, "but I'm telling you something different. Democracy is a way to transfer control of the government from one group to another in a peaceful fashion, without all the upheavals and power struggles that you find in dictatorships."

"Dictatorships don't represent the will of the people."

"Well, democracy doesn't necessarily do that, either. In between elections, the voters have very little control over the government. Politicians even break election promises sometimes, right?"

"If they do, we can elect somebody else."

"But maybe the damage has already been done. Or maybe the politician is giving us lip service instead of delivering real results. Face it, most people don't have time to keep track of what's going on in Congress from day to day."

"But congressmen represent the people," said Arthur Dudley. "That's what we elect them for."

The other students squirmed in their seats.

"Fine. Can we just…get out of this loop, Mr. Dudley? We have other things to cover."

Popovich hurried to the next topic, but he had lost his stride, and his audience along with it. The students had slid back into their customary mental torpor, and would henceforth be impervious to all outside stimuli except the mention of grades. Wrapping up his lecture, Popovich reminded students that late papers would be marked down. This remark provoked a mild flutter of neuronal activity in the room, and then the class was over.

A few students waited to see him. One bright kid named Howard wanted to combine Jefferson, Hobbes, and Rousseau in one paper (he didn't know how yet). Another presented a note for some future doctor's appointments (Popovich would later forget and mark him absent for those days). A pretty and stylish girl named Bertha said, "I get your point, Professor. Democracy is like some kind of objective system we all agree on, even if the politicians some-times sleaze around it. Isn't that right?"

"Exactly," Popovich said.

"I thought so!" she said excitedly. Her youthful enthusiasm seemed at odds with her sophisticated outfit. Popovich would have liked to chat with her for few moments, but the ominous presence of Arthur Dudley loomed in the background. Bertha saw him, but she showed no emotion whatsoever.

Arthur Dudley said, "You don't believe that a government should represent the people?"

"Of course I believe it should. I also believe that nobody in the world should be sick or hungry." Popovich immediately regretted his glibness.

"That's what I want to do my paper on, how democracy is the best system because it represents the will of the people."

"I would prefer you didn't. It's not…analytical enough."

"But that's the topic I want to do."

"It's unworthy of your talents." Popovich smiled falsely. Being rude to students was forbidden, but there were absolutely no restrictions on hypocrisy.

"What's wrong with my topic?" Arthur Dudley insisted.

"It's just too clichéd," Popovich said, snapping shut the locks on his satchel and heading out the door. Outside, the autumnal sun fell on the dazzling river and the sounds of rock and roll wafted over the campus, coming from giant speakers along fraternity row. Popovich went to Guild Hall to pick up his mail and found two notes in his mailbox. The first note, from the Chairman of the Department, promised him an embossed nameplate for his office door. The other one, from the Vice-Chairman, Allen Druwart, requested to see him. It couldn't possibly be good news. The Department never had any good news. Popovich went to Druwart's office to get it over with as quickly as possible.

"Stan! Come in, sit down." They shook hands.

"I'll get right to the point. It's about your dissertation. The Department feels that it's time for you to get on the stick."

"I'm on the stick, Allen. I can feel I'm on the stick."

"That's good, Stan, because they want you to finish and defend by the end of the semester."

"By the end of the semester? Come on, even if I finished it tomorrow, I doubt if I could get a defense committee together by December. I mean, everybody on a defense committee has to read the thing…then there's the schedules, everybody with their classes, their conferences…just getting them all together in one room…"

Druwart leaned back in his chair and considered what Popovich had just said. "OK, look, I'll tell you what. If you have a completed dissertation by the start of next semester—I mean a manuscript, a diskette, that you can hand over to the Department—then maybe, just maybe, we can hold out until spring for the actual defense."

Popovich blinked like he'd just missed a collision. "Thank you."

"If the dissertation is really good," added Druwart quickly.

"Oh, it is."

"Well," he said, with an air of closure, "we all appreciate what a dedicated teacher you are and how much the students like you, so we're all pulling for you to get this dissertation business behind you."

"Me, too. I mean, I will," said Popovich.

Later at home, the conversation throbbed in his memory and did not go away. Druwart bothered him. He was younger than Popovich, and already possessed everything Popovich lacked—a secure job, a wife, a little boy, an office with a view of the river. True, he had never had an original idea in his life; his scholarship was a strictly a garage sale of other people's work. So Popovich reminded himself, often, as he sat in his neat, orderly study surrounded by floor-to-ceiling bookshelves. But even as he tried to console himself with thoughts of Druwart's intellectual mediocrity, another part of him whispered that drowning himself in this kind of solace was no better than drinking cheap booze, and tasted like it, too.

October began badly. In the first class on the first day of the month, the first hand up was Arthur Dudley's.

"I want to do my term paper on how democracy represents the people," he said. He didn't speak angrily or resentfully. Rather, he had the look of a whipped cur, even though Popovich hadn't yet addressed a single word to him.

"You can do a paper on democracy, Mr. Dudley, but not on that topic. Why not try another approach?"

"I want to do the approach I talked to you about last week."

Exasperated, Popovich threw his hands in the air. The bright kid, Howard, turned to Arthur Dudley and said, "Look, dude, if he doesn't want you to do it, don't keep pushing it, OK?" He turned to Popovich with a mirthless grin. "Sorry. You were saying?" Popovich wanted to hug Howard, but settled for a quick nod of the head.

At the end of the period, Arthur Dudley came up to the front desk. "Why are you against democracy?" he asked.

Elegant Bertha, today wearing a cloche hat, paused at the door. "Who says the professor is against democracy?"

"My father says," replied Arthur Dudley.

A slight chill traveled across Popovich's skin. No windows were open.

"Your father is wrong," said Bertha, scowling at both of them, Arthur and Popovich, perhaps to make it clear that she was only venting an opinion, and not taking sides. Defeated, Arthur Dudley picked up his books and walked out without looking at anybody.

Back at the Department, Popovich's mailbox yielded the usual load of junk: unwanted textbooks, announcements for boring campus events and another note from Druwart. Another note! What new deadline nightmare awaited him? Druwart was in his office, slicing letters open with a slim silver knife.

"Stan, quick question. You have an Arthur Dudley in your class?"

"Yeah, unfortunately."

"Unfortunately is right. Yesterday his father called just about everybody in the university except the janitors to complain about you."

"What's the problem? That I didn't like his son's term paper topic?"

"No, it's...you somehow give the impression that you're against democracy."

"I question democracy. That's a lot different. Is asking questions now considered a hostile act?"

"Apparently so, in the prevailing, I don't know, climate?" Frowning, Druwart said, "Look, we're not about to tell you what to say in class, just be careful, OK?"

"I'll be careful."

"Kid gloves, you know what I mean?"

"Gotcha."

"I knew you'd understand!"

Luckily, the desk that stood between them prevented Druwart from clapping his hand on Popovich's suddenly delicate shoulder.

After the conversation with Druwart, hell seemed to be securely fastened, but a week later, it broke loose again. Popovich spent the weekend trying to work on his dissertation, but his mind kept drifting to Arthur Dudley. He called up Catherine Vanderburgh to talk about it. She was one of his more empathetic—and emphatic—colleagues from the Department. "The problem is," said Popovich, "is that he's a dimwit, but I'm afraid to flunk him, because he'll take it like some kind of personal vendetta."

"If he deserves to fail, fail him!" she almost shouted. "Never mind what he thinks, he obviously doesn't belong in a university. "

"But he doesn't seem to know that. It's like…he's too stupid to understand how stupid he is."

"Don't worry about him, just finish your chapter, honey. And right now I have to finish mine.

"OK, thanks, see you next week."

Catherine was already working on her second book.

Come Tuesday, and the next meeting with the Arthur Dudley class, Popovich noticed an unmistakable mood of discontent when he entered the classroom. True, it was a gloomy day; rain pummeled the window panes and drove yellow leaves into swirling gutters. Perhaps the malaise he sensed was caused by the weather, or by the impending threat of midterm exams, or perhaps, in some mysteriously indirect way, by stock market activity or atomic testing in China. But he didn't think so. He attempted levity. "Hellooo, anybody alive out there? Anybody have a pulse?" No answer from the class. "Guess not," he said, erasing the board. He put down a few words: concrete, abstract, politics, ideology. With a discreet cough, he began to talk about ideology as moral justification. Somebody raised a hand. "Yes?"

"Is democracy also an ideology? A justification?"

Popovich failed to sense the imminent danger. "Yes," he said, "certainly, from one point of view, it definitely is. When you claim that democracy is representative, you don't explain anything, you only justify."

"So again," said the student who had raised his hand, "you're claiming that democracy is a fraud, that it's a crock, and we're all fools for believing in it?"

"What? I never said anything like that! Come on, where've you been all semester?"

"I've been right here. I just didn't hear what you were really saying until now, that's all."

The student gave a nonchalant little shrug, as if the case were closed, and there was nothing left to get excited about. But Popovich was just beginning to find things to get excited about. He addressed the student in his best professorial manner, which was the safest way to assert his superiority. "OK, then just tell me one thing. How did you come to find out what I was really saying?" He put so much sarcastic emphasis on really that some people giggled. "Was it something I said? Or did you actually read something?"

The student's lower lip protruded defiantly. He made a vague gesture. "Excuse me?" said Popovich. "I can't hear you."

"I just figured it out, that's all." That said, the student folded his arms on his desk and pretended to go to sleep. Popovich was furious, but was afraid he would lose the class entirely if he didn't keep his temper in check. He paced in front of the board. "Unfortunately, I think there's been some kind of misunderstanding. And I don't really know how to deal with it, because it's never happened to me before."

A pony-tailed girl blurted out, "Really? It never happened to you before?" "No." said Popovich quietly. "Why, has someone told you otherwise?" Howard turned and pointed at Arthur Dudley. "Ask him! Ask his father!"

"Excuse me?"

Howard leaned back in his chair, grinned, and shook his head, as if recalling some irresistible private joke. He refused to meet Popovich's eyes. Vexed and frustrated, Popovich blundered once again, felt himself blundering, knew full well he was blundering, but couldn't control the forward rush of his impatience. "All right, people. Let me just ask one single question. How many people here know Mr. Dudley's father?"

This question caused a visible stir in the classroom, some sharply-drawn breaths, a few grimaces. Arthur Dudley raised his hand, but Popovich ignored him. "OK, class, let's try this! First, everybody take out a sheet of paper. On it, I want you to write down whether or not you know Mr. Dudley's father. Don't sign your name. Disguise your handwriting if you want. Then fold the paper in two and pass it up front."

Arthur Dudley was now waving his hand in the air like crazy. Perhaps it would be prudent to allow him to speak.

"Yes, Mr. Dudley?"

"Do I also have to write down that I know my father?"

A small wave of nervous laughter swept the class.

"Do what you like. This isn't a quiz," said Popovich, feeling suddenly exhausted. "It's not graded."

The entire class relaxed. The papers rustled from hand to hand and piled up on the teacher's desk. Popovich turned in place like a chained animal, not knowing what to do next, until at last he saw the words Concrete and Abstract on the board. He commenced lecturing on the difference between the two terms, making sure to keep the entire discussion as abstract as possible. He ended the class early.

On their way out of class, some students glanced at him with pity, some with ill-concealed disdain. Arthur Dudley ignored him completely; so did Howard. Trying to appear casual, Popovich reached for the folded papers and opened them one by one. I know Arthur's father. I know Mr. Dudley. I know Arthur Dudley's father. And so on. All but two or three students in the class replied affirmatively. I know of Arthur Dudley's father. That "of," how should he take that? He sat down. He could not think. He decided that he must be stunned. That was it. He was stunned.

Only Bertha still remained in the classroom, holding her books in her arms, looking at him sympathetically. She wore an antique tailored suit with a string of small pearls. Hard to say if the pearls were genuine or not.

"I know Arthur Dudley's father," she volunteered.

"How do you know him? Are you a friend of Arthur's?"

She laughed. "Arthur? No way. It's just that his father, Mr. Dudley, came up to the dorms this week to see Arthur and ended up, like, talking to lots and lots of students."

Popovich clutched the desk to keep himself from whirling away. "What do you mean? Why was he talking to students? What was he talking about?"

"Oh, I don't know, about themselves, and about, you know, like, whatever they want. He made a lot of money in the construction business and then he ran for State Assembly and lost, but he, like, wants to get involved in public issues. At least that's what he said."

"Public issues, huh?"

"Actually, I think he said great public issues." Bertha blushed a little, as if she were repeating naughty words.

"Great public issues like his son's term paper, huh?"

"How should I know?…I mean, you asked me."

Popovich stood up and looked into Bertha's bright brown eyes. "Look, I am deeply grateful for everything you just told me. Believe me, Miss Emerson, I had no idea at all what was going on."

At these words, Bertha's expression fluttered between nervousness and pleasure.

"You can call me Bertha," she said, and left.

Popovich gathered the folded papers in his hands and scattered them in the general direction of the trash bin. Avoiding the Department, he went directly home, tossed his satchel aside, and turned on the classical radio station. For some time he lay on his couch suspended between sleep and waking. He got up and forced himself to sit at his word processor, but could not keep his mind on his dissertation. If he jumped in his car and drove one hundred miles right now, he could be ringing his former girlfriend's doorbell by midnight, and undoing her buttons with trembling fingers by one, maybe one-thirty, but in the morning she would mope at his departure, making him feel abrupt and heartless. And Popovich certainly had enough bad feelings to contend with as it was.

When the Arthur Dudley class met again, on Thursday, Popovich was prepared to fight, if necessary, but he encountered no resistance. The class was merely demoralized. Their faces, insofar as he could read them, conveyed only the desire to be elsewhere.

Popovich wasn't accustomed to indifference. He had always prided himself on getting the students involved, drawing them out, making them participate. He wanted to scream at the class. He wanted to tell them that he was an excellent teacher. Yes, he sometimes got postcards from students who had left the university years ago! The daughter of a former U.S. senator had taken his class and loved it!

But Popovich kept all this to himself, because he was afraid that any attempt to justify himself might make him look more, not less, contemptible. When he called on students, they answered grudgingly, in a bored, faintly derisory manner, but without crossing over into open rudeness or defiance. This sneaky insolence not only caused Popovich pain, but frustration as well. He had imagined that he and the class were headed for a decisive event, a blow-up of some kind, which would be followed by reconciliation and maybe a renewed respect on both sides. Indeed, exactly this scenario had occurred before, with individual students. Of course, sometimes a student developed a secret grudge against him and held it to the bitter end.

Now he had an entire class like that.

He tried not to dwell on it. He forced himself to work at his dissertation but would often find himself staring at his word processor with a stubbornly blank mind. He ran into Druwart once or twice in the corridors of Guild Hall, but did not yield to the temptation to complain about the class. Druwart's eyebrows went up and down, as if he were also suppressing the temptation to say something. Whenever they met, the air between them thickened with Significant Glances, and sometimes a few Inquisitive Gazes from nosy bystanders.

Fortunately, there was no need to be circumspect around Catherine Vanderburgh. As they took turns at the copying machine in the Department, Popovich asked her if she had ever heard of Arthur Dudley's father.

"Yes, I think I have, as a matter of fact. Isn't he that guy who goes around the dorms talking to students?"

"That's him! What do you know about him?"

"Just that. He talks to students."

"Well, he called Allen and god knows who else to complain about me. His son is in my class—that's the idiot I was telling you about, remember?"

"His son is that guy? What a joke."

"I don't know, I'm worried about failing him, that's the truth. I'm seriously considering just…pushing him through with a passing grade."

"Don't tell me you're going to let that man intimidate you? You can't, Stan. Suppose every parent who didn't like his kid's grades started throwing his weight around? Please!"

"Yeah, you're right. It's a matter of integrity," said Popovich feebly.

Somehow the word integrity sounded ominous to his own ears. It wasn't like decency or empathy, which were common, garden-variety virtues that required very little effort. Integrity came at a price. The word reeked of sacrifice.

On his way home, he stopped off at a popular campus restaurant to have a sandwich and saw his student Bertha. She was waitressing there. She greeted him with a cheery smile.

"Just sit in that section over there," she said, "and I'll be right over."

A few minutes later she came by and said, "Tell you a secret? I'm like not really supposed to work here. They serve alcohol, and I'm not twenty-one yet. I had to lie about my age."

"Lying is the first principle of politics, so I approve," said Popovich.

"I just love politics and want to major in it." With an embarrassed grin, she added quickly, "I'll bet all the students tell you that."

"No, they usually tell me that they find politics incredibly boring."

Bertha leaned in closer. "I saw Mr. Dudley again. Arthur's father."

"You did?"

She crinkled her nose. "I can't take him. But look, it's pretty busy here, so why don't you give me your order?"

It was November. Wet skies, cold wind, darkness closing in earlier. The students turned in the first draft of their term papers. Bertha did something ambitious with Plato's Republic. At the end of class, Popovich —as was his policy—returned several first drafts because they weren't long enough to merit even a preliminary critique. Arthur Dudley's paper was one of these. It was called, "Democracy: The People's Voice." Popovich asked him to stay after class for a moment.

"First of all, this paper is only four and a half pages. I said the first draft should be at least eight. Second, it's the wrong topic. I told you explicitly that this topic was not a good one, didn't I?"

Arthur Dudley stood before his desk holding a small backpack and wearing a baseball cap, warm-up outfit, and a bright orange windbreaker. His eyes were large, puppy-like. He seemed to ponder Popovich's question.

"I like this topic," he said at last.

"Look, there's nothing wrong with this topic. It's fine. But it s a dead horse. Don't keep beating it. OK?"

Looking unhappy, Arthur Dudley threw his backpack over his shoulder and left the classroom. Popovich thought about running after him, but what could he say that he hadn't already said and said again? He wasn't in class the following Tuesday. Funny, but up till now he had never missed a single one of Popovich's lectures, even though his fellow students were cutting out in record numbers. These days, less than half the roster showed up for any given class period.

When Popovich went to Guild Hall to check his mail, Allen Druwart pounced on him.

"Uh, Stan, do have a minute? Could you step into my office?"

He herded Popovich ahead of him and pulled the door shut when they were both inside.

"Is it Arthur Dudley again?"

"His father," said Druwart. "Sit down, won't you?"

"If it's about his son's term paper, forget it. I asked for eight pages and he only gave me four and a half."

"He didn't mention any term paper." Druwart's face tightened. "This is something else."

"Oh yeah? What?

"He wants to sit in on one of your lectures."

"Sit in on my lecture? What for?" Druwart didn't say anything. "Absolutely not."

"Stan, think it over. It's your decision, but please think about it first."

"No, no, and no! It's a matter of principle. If he wants to sit in on my class, let him matriculate and pay for the course like everybody else. This man is not qualified to sit in judgment of my teaching."

Druwart lifted his arms in a conciliatory gesture, as if to embrace Popovich's righteous wrath. "Just think about what you're saying."

"I am thinking. Now if you want to sit in on my class, that's a different story."

"Me? Oh, no. I'm busy. I have my own classes. Sorry, but no."

"Or any other faculty member in the Department."

"That's for you to arrange," said Druwart quickly. "I'm only conveying this Mr. Dudley's request. Naturally, you have every right to refuse. I personally think it would be for the best if you just let this guy, whoever he is, sit in the back of the class for a while, so he can see for himself you're not teaching the kids how to mix gasoline bombs, or whatever the hell he thinks you're doing."

"Would you let him into one of your classes?"

"Yes…I think I would. I mean, the man is a real nuisance, I'm not saying he's not a royal pain in the rectum." Druwart swung round in his mobile chair. For a moment he stared away, trying to see the mental tangle. "Yes, I would let him sit in. Hey, why not?"

"Tell you what. I'll think it over," said Popovich untruthfully.

"I'm sure you'll come to the right decision."

Wind stripped the last yellow leaves from the trees and rippled the lead-colored river. The campus geared up for the end of the semester. Activity shifted from dormitories and frat houses to libraries, labs, and all-night study lounges. The term papers that Popovich took home were dull and banal; only Howard and Bertha seemed at all interested in what they were writing about. Arthur Dudley insisted on pursuing his favorite topic. If he had done even a mediocre job with it, Popovich would have given him a C and moved on, but the paper was so ungrammatical and disjointed that he was forced to fail it regardless of the content.

The campus was mostly deserted when Popovich brought his semester grade sheet to Guild Hall. Among the Christmas ornaments and notices offering holiday travel packages for students, one poster caught his eye: College Democracy Initiative. Join Now! For details, contact the following organizers….

One of the names was Arthur Dudley. Popovich was less surprised at finding Arthur Dudley's name linked with the sacred cause of College Democracy (whatever that might be) than by the idea of Arthur Dudley organizing anything whatsoever. Most days he couldn't even organize a shave.

After handing in his grades, Popovich strolled over to the restaurant where Bertha might still be working, if she hadn't already left town for the holidays.

And he was in luck; there she was, gliding between the chrome and plastic booths.

Bertha appeared glad to see him. She was working straight through to Christmas Eve because she needed the money. She wouldn't be traveling home until Christmas Day. Popovich complimented her on her term paper and told her she had gotten an A. She was pleased, but not surprised. He ordered a sandwich and when he was through she brought him a piece of chocolate cake "on the house," probably without informing the house of its own generosity. When he asked for the check, she began to weep. Popovich was astonished.

"Are you busy? Can I talk to you for a minute?" she asked.

"Of course!"

"Not here. Just wait a moment, it's almost my break time—I'll tell them I'm going out for a while."

She came back wearing her coat and they walked into the blustery cold.

"Where do you want to go?" asked Popovich.

"We can go into the Red Lion."

"I don't want to be around other people," she said, touching her eyes with a glove.

"How about my car? It's parked in the lot behind Guild Hall."

As they walked along, Bertha stared at the ground. "Did you fail Arthur Dudley? No, don't tell me, it's confidential."

"He's a terrible writer. I don't know how he survived freshman English." They got into Popovich's tiny car and sat side by side, awkwardly claustrophobic in their bundles of winter clothing.

"If I tell you something, will you promise to never ever tell anybody else? No matter what?"

"I promise."

"OK. Do you know who Professor Druwart is?"

Popovich nodded. He felt a chill creeping under his skin.

"I had him for a class this semester. I…I slept with him three times."

Popovich reeled. It was a blow, a stab to the vitals, a fierce attack of — what? Of jealousy? Was this rage about her, or about Druwart? He suppressed a fleeting urge to punch something.

"Are you pregnant?"

She shook her head and smiled through her tears, which now coursed over her pink cheeks. "No, thank God for that. He's got a wife and a kid. If anything like that happened, I would be like in the middle of this huge uproar."

"Hey, don't worry, I won't tell anybody." Popovich looked at her. She did not appear to be despondent. At worse, she might be a little miserable, but she was mostly just overwrought. She had put herself through too many big emotions too quickly. Popovich put his arms around her. Even as he did so, he wondered if this very scene might scandalize some casual passerby: a professor hugging a student in his car in an almost deserted parking lot. Certainly, it would be just his luck to be caught and punished for Druwart's crime. He withdrew his arms. "There's some tissue in the glove compartment," he said.

"I'll bet my makeup is a mess." He nodded empathically.

She repaired her face in the rearview mirror. "I have to go back to work now."

He drove her to the restaurant. "Well, Merry Christmas," she said.

"You, too. Have a good holiday."

Shaking with indignation, upset by a desire that he never wished to acknowledge, Popovich went straight home to his study and tried to pick up his dissertation where he had last left it off. He was sick and tired of it. Over the next three weeks he quickly slapped together the last two chapters without caring if they were any good. So the work of years ended abruptly in a mood of disinterest and anti-climax. He sent copies to his advisor and to the other faculty members who had been persuaded or coerced into validating his doctoral aspirations. The formal defense was scheduled for March.

On an icy white day in late January, shortly before classes resumed for the new semester, he went to Guild Hall carrying a manuscript of his completed dissertation to give to Druwart. He would have preferred to hand it over to the Department Chairman, or to any of his other colleagues, or, indeed, to a rabid leper, but he had no choice. Druwart chaired the Faculty Committee and didn't let anything go behind his back. He automatically opposed anything that he hadn't been among the first to hear about.

The Department bustled with new-semester activity. Druwart looked surprised and displeased to see Popovich, but scurried around his desk to close the door behind him as he entered.

"Hi, Allen, how was your holiday?"

"Fine. I was going to put a note in your box, but you just saved me the trouble."

"Well, I've got some news."

"So do I," said Druwart brusquely. "We're giving you a lighter course load this semester."

"What do you mean, lighter load?"

"One class, Stan, we're giving you one single class this semester. Sorry about that, but that's the way it has to be, I'm afraid."

"I don't get it."

Druwart perched on the edge of his desk. "It's your...dissertation, Stan. The Faculty Committee felt you've been dragging out this doctoral business too long. It's been, what..."

"My dissertation is finished. That's my news. I've got it with me, and my defense is set up for March." He paused for reaction. "If you don't believe me, ask my advisor."

"Stan, look, I'm really sorry, but it's too late. You should have defended in November, December. Didn't we go over this together, right here?"

"Yeah, we did, and you said it would be OK if I defended this spring."

"I said maybe it would be OK. But I'm afraid it's just not. Not anymore."

Popovich couldn't think, couldn't reply.

"You better start applying for new jobs," Druwart continued. "We won't be keeping you after this semester."

Popovich looked up at the clock, heard it ticking, heard the sound of footsteps and voices outside, watched Druwart swaying as he leaned against his desk.

"It's about Arthur Dudley, isn't it? No, I mean Arthur Dudley's father. He's been putting the heat on, right? Phone calls, what else?"

"Well, I'll say this much—that didn't help you one bit."

"Don't bullshit me, this has nothing to do with my dissertation and everything to do with bad publicity. It's all about public relations, isn't it? You sacrificed me for public relations."

"Not at all."

"Oh yes, oh yes, you did. I can smell it from here."

"Stan, Stan, what happened to you? You used to be such a good teacher!"

"Fuck you, I'm still a good teacher."

Druwart opened the door. "I think you better leave."

Popovich got up and walked to the door, stopped, and turned around. "Oh by the way, did you have a student in your class last semester, a Miss Bertha Emerson?"

Druwart froze. His eyes grew wide.

Popovich smiled brightly. "Name ring a bell? Or do you want to check your roster?"

"I told you to leave!" roared Druwart.

"People everywhere are talking about what a slimy, sleazy little..."

Druwart slammed the door in his face, causing everybody in the busy corridor to stop and stare. They saw Popovich standing in front of the door, red-faced and grinning with rage. Then they turned away, embarrassed.

In a daze, Popovich walked across campus without direction or purpose.

He needed the air to clear his head; even freezing air would do. As he approached Main Hall, he saw a crowd of students lined up in the cold, moving around and clapping their gloves to keep warm. He looked around and noticed that the buildings in the vicinity were splashed with colorful posters: Kick-Off Rally! College Democracy Initiative. James Dudley, Speaker. Free Tickets Available in Main Hall Today.

Popovich turned to the nearest group of students. "What's all this about?"

"Really cool," said one, nodding.

"You ought to check it out," said another.

"Sure, thanks for the information." He decided to go home and call Catherine Vanderburgh, but as it turned out, she was definitely not in the frame of mind to listen to his problems or anybody else's.

"I'm on the edge of hysteria!" she said. "I've been frantically revising my lesson plans for the next two weeks!"

"How come?"

"How come? I'll tell you how come—that horrible Dudley character is going to sit in on one of my classes! I mean nobody has actually observed me in the classroom since I was a teaching assistant!"

"Why did you give him permission to sit in on your class then?"

Her voice turned hard. "Sorry, Stan, I can't really talk now. Let's get together some time." She hung up.

Popovich never called her back, and though they ran into each other once or twice on campus during the semester, they only exchanged quick greetings and moved on. He and Druwart never spoke to each other again. They didn't even make eye contact. Druwart was too frightened and Popovich was too ashamed. Ashamed that he had betrayed Bertha's trust in him for a moment's chance to be spiteful. She was only person who'd been honest with him.

He saw her just once more on campus. It was late in the afternoon, immediately following his only—and very last—class. Rain fell and wind gusted, but from a milder quarter of the earth than it had during winter. They went to the Red Lion and had a beer, and talked for an hour about Plato's Republic and the whole concept of utopia.

More Than One Condition

The other day I went into a drugstore to pick up some dandruff shampoo. Though my hair dwindles, my dandruff output remains steady. The remaining hairs must be working at it harder and harder. Anyway, I guess I was more than usually absent-minded that day, because I simply put the bottle of shampoo into my pocket. Then I notice a sales clerk watching me, so I immediately jerk the bottle out of my pocket with a silly, embarrassed grin. Then I see to my surprise that no sales clerk is watching me. In fact, nobody is watching me at all. What I took for a squad of undercover cops is really a rack of sunglasses on sale. In a flash, I realize what happened. I just experienced an episode of kleptomania followed by a paranoid hallucination. It was a textbook case.

In the next store, a supermarket, I have another attack of paranoid kleptomania. I impulsively stick a package of pork chops under my coat, then immediately feel intense remorse and fear of arrest. I'm compelled to return the item immediately, but before I can put the chops back, an employee in white apron appears behind me. I dart into the next aisle, but it's crowded with shoppers.

And the next aisle also. I pace around nervously, too scared to let anybody see me get rid of my stolen goods.

Finally I go next door to a bookstore, and there, in the darkest and most deserted corner—the poetry section—I slip the package of pork chops in between The Wasteland and the poems of Emily Dickinson, figuring that if anybody smells anything, they'll blame it on T.S. Eliot.

On my way out, I steal a copy of Oliver Twist, which I leave in a liquor store between the gin and vermouth. The owner of the liquor store is a suspicious type, watching me all the time. I can only keep reaching for bottles and then pulling my hand back suddenly. I finally decide to buy a bottle of wine but he won't sell it to me.

It is slowly becoming apparent that a man with my particular compulsions shouldn't be hanging around shopping centers. I decide to visit a friend. As we drink some iced tea and sit around chatting, I surreptitiously pick up little objects off his coffee table and tuck them in my shirt. Every time he gets up to answer the phone or fetch more guacamole, I replace the objects. When he discovers that his glass of iced tea is missing, I get down on hands and knees and pretend to find it under the couch. He is a little upset. "What the hell are you doing?" he bellows. "What kind of stupid game is this?"

"I've become a kleptomaniac. Please, please forgive me!" He can only gape at me in surprise and shock.

"I'm guilty and I'm tormented with remorse," I say. I pull a small clock and a couple of coasters out of my pocket and put them back on the coffee table where they belong. "You see," I say, "I'm both a kleptomaniac and paranoid."

He thinks about his for a moment. "That really sucks, man." It's a logical inference, but I don't like his tone of voice.

"It's better than being an arsonist and a nymphomaniac," I say.

"You keep my mother out of this," he says.

And that little sentence sets me to telling him about my own parents. My father was a policeman and my mother was a shoplifter. For him it was arrest at first sight.

He courted her all the way to court. He told her, "If you don't marry me I'll testify against you in court and you'll get ninety days."

"Some choice," she said. "Ninety days or life." And so my mother gave up a promising career in the glamorous field of price-tag switching in order to get married.

At this point in my reminiscences my friend gently takes me by the scruff of the neck and tells me to go home and try to stay out of trouble. So I go home. But I'm still feeling kleptomaniacal, so I try stealing from myself. I start lifting objects from my living room and sticking them in my pocket. But I don't really enjoy this activity very much. For a thief, it's like masturbating.

The moves are the same, but there's no relationship there. Indeed, you can do anything you want with your own stuff except steal it. Which goes to show that ownership has its limits. We tend to think that the rich can do anything, but they can't steal their own stuff. Luckily, they can generally count on the regular staff to do it without being asked. Poor people don't have old, faithful servants to rob them; they have to depend on complete strangers.

At this point, I decide that I'll just fake it. I call the police station and report a burglary. A policeman comes to my door.

"What'd you lose?" he says.

I name several items, such as a phone, a gold neck chain, and an expensive watch—objects which are even now bulging in my pockets.

"See anybody lurking around here?" says the cop, flipping open his notebook.

I say yes and proceed to describe myself—my height, my age, my distinguishing features. The policeman gives me hard looks as he jots down the information. Finally he closes the notebook and growls from the bottom of his throat, suggesting that he has trouble expressing anger without the aid of a nightstick.

The door slams. Then I realize that I'm holding the policeman's hat. Shit!

Now I'm in trouble. What do you do with a hot cop cap? Bury it? Burn it? Suppose he comes back for it? I only have one thing going for me in this whole situation. I'm white. Everything else pretty much sucks.

I get an idea. I go outside and walk around looking for somebody weaker than me. Finally I see a kid spray-painting dirty words on parked cars. I say, "The word shit only has one h, Picasso." He flips me a very impolite finger. I grab him and shove the cop's hat on his head. "You arrogant tadpole," I say. "I want you to remove this haberdashery from the vicinity of my responsibility immediately." It's either my impressive choice of words or the arm lock around his windpipe that finally persuades him to take the hat. I let him go and he runs off.

Instantly, I feel a blessed relief. All the shimmering delusions of guilt, remorse, and paranoia vanish and I experience the great new sensation of being a normal person. I am overwhelmed by normal thoughts and normal opinions. I vote for a politician who promises to make medical insurance unavailable, college education unaffordable, our lifestyle unsustainable, and the earth uninhabitable. And the beautiful part of the plan is that the money saved from these cutbacks would be given to the very rich in the form of tax breaks. It all makes perfect sense to me for the first time. I can easily solve my financial problem by winning the lottery.

As I am rejoicing in my new found freedom, a cop car pulls up and a policeman without a hat comes out and puts handcuffs on me. In the back seat, I see the young graffiti artist. He is crying and pointing to me, saying, "That's the one, that's the one who tried to kill me."

"You're in big trouble now," says the officer. "I didn't try to kill him, your majesty."

I know he's only a cop, but it doesn't hurt to flatter people a little in these circumstances

"Your majesty, huh?" says the cop. "I don't like that kind of sarcasm. You're under arrest for insulting an officer of the law. In addition, I'm charging you with theft, assault, perjury, and several counts of shoplifting. a real nut job, mister! You need to see Doctor Twinkle Toes."

But I'm absolutely normal in all respects!" I say. Now he believes me even less.

I'm awaiting trial now, so I have to be careful and avoid stealing things. So I'm stealing words instead of things. For instance, this story is really "The Snows of Kilimanjaro" by Ernest Hemingway, but I've rearranged the words very carefully so nobody will notice.

I'm With the Band

In 1980, me and my old friend Paul moved into the East Village and discovered that dark energy called Punk. Young people with piercings and tattoos, out in the streets, drinking, taking pills, picking fights. They mostly came into the city from Queens and Long Island on weekends. Anger was in fashion and rage was all the rage.

Paul and I were already too old to be considered punks, but we knew them well because we were both working in a bar called Pete's Tropical Fish. It didn't have a liquor license or a single permit from the city. It was open all night. Paul was the star bartender. Women noticed Paul's green eyes and his air of brooding. Actually, he was just trying to think. Thinking did not come easy to Paul. There were too many distractions. He was always going out of his way to avoid distractions, until he met the greatest distraction he would ever know, Mirabella.

This happened when Paul got home one morning at the usual half past three. It was always a little dangerous at that hour to walk along junkie-infested Tomkins Square Park, but Paul was broad-shouldered and moved fast. When he entered the apartment he found Joshua—his roommate and drummer in their band, which was called Truth Decay—sitting with a stoned grin on his face and a cigarette in his hand that seemed to be burning his fingers. Two women were snorting coke on the kitchen table and jabbering in Spanish. One was beautiful and skinny and dressed entirely in black. The other one was chubby and dressed entirely in black.

Joshua said, pointing at the skinny woman, "That's Mirabella. The other I forget, I think her name is Gorda. They're from Argentina."

Paul said, "You're stinking drunk, man."

Joshua turned to the women and said, "Chicas, es mi amigo Paul, el bajista del grupo."

The two women swarmed over Paul and kissed him on both cheeks. He extricated himself as gently as possible. The chunky one said something in Spanish. They laughed.

"She said that you must be the best-looking bass player on Tenth Street."

"Just East Tenth," said Paul. "West Tenth is gay, and those guys always look fabulous."

Mirabella began tugging at Paul's sleeve. "You want to try coca? Very good quality. Your head will go around and around. Dancing." She twirled on one heel and knocked an open beer bottle off the table with her elbow. It fell and spilled on a leather jacket that was lying on the floor. The chunky woman said something sharp in Spanish to Mirabella, who said to Joshua, "She wants me to stop dancing."

Joshua said, "Stop dancing now!"

"No! I am free!" she said.

"No! No!" said Joshua in a panic. The neighbors had warned him about drumming too late. He said, "Don't dance here! No baile aquí!"

Paul sat down. He could see his face in the mirror on the table, looming behind little white lines. He picked up a rolled-up dollar bill, stuck one end in the right nostril, and vacuumed up some powder. He went to the refrigerator and dug a beer out of the mess. Then some more lines, this time through the left nostril. The next thing he knew, the sun was up, Joshua and Gorda were gone, Mirabella was copying the number of the telephone (dial, wall-mounted), and his head was too heavy to lift off the table.

We held our weekly rehearsal in a rented sound studio on 30th Street.

Paul and Joshua always warmed up by trying to reproduce the booming reggae rhythms of Robbie Shakespeare and Sly Dunbar, but they were fatigued and kept losing the beat. Joey Purple—so called because he dyed his hair that color— was the group's song writer and musical director. He was picking up various instruments, now a sax, now a flute, now an electric guitar, to fill in the gaps. He had red rabbit eyes and skin problems from working with industrial solvents at a giant art supply store on Canal Street. His brain had been affected, perhaps permanently, by carelessly inhaling toxic fumes. But his music had gotten much more interesting.

I was the least proficient musician in the band. I just strummed a big acoustic guitar or riffed on the chords. I played whatever Joey Purple told me to play. In fact, his instructions always allowed broad freedom of interpretation. "It should sound like orange juice with pulp." Or else he'd say, "The first part should be Memphis, Tennessee, and the second part should be more like Memphis, Egypt."

Paul appeared to be brooding. Thinking was evidently a special effort for him today. There was a knock on the door, which was massive and reinforced with steel plates. We looked at each other. We had agreed that nobody but the band was allowed in the studio during rehearsals.

"Who's there?" yelled Joey Purple. "The door's unlocked!" More knocking. "I said it's unlocked!"

Joey Purple opened the door for a slender, elegant woman who wore a floppy white hat, big round dark glasses and a tight little black top and black jeans. It was Mirabella. She carried a large pouch with abstract Japanese ocean waves appliquéd on it.

Joshua sighed. "OK, I suck. I gave her this address last night."

Mirabella lifted her sunglasses, looked around and said, "What a heavy door! Are you afraid of somebody?"

We're afraid of interruptions like this one," said Paul. "What makes you think you can barge in like you own the place?"

The harshness in his voice silenced the room. She lowered her dark glasses to cover her eyes.

I rushed in to smooth over the awkward pause. "You wanna hear something very interesting? This was once a factory," I said.

"Why is that interesting?" said Mirabella.

"Once upon a time things were manufactured in New York," said Joey Purple. "Now the city just makes symbolic stuff like junk bonds, Tony Awards, and fashion statements. The city used to be materialist, now it's conceptual. "

"I have a concept too," I said. "Let's rehearse."

"Is OK that I stay here and draw?" asked Mirabella, pulling from her pouch a sketchpad and some conté crayons.

"Yes, if you shut up," said Joshua. "That goes for everyone. If you feel the urge to talk, try to keep it to yourself, OK? Paul, Joey, ready? Harvey, ready to rock?" I nodded. "I'm going to count off for 'Point Blank Headshot.' And-a-one-and-a-two-and-a-three-and-a…"

We went through our usual set, starting and stopping, trying to tighten it and focus every song. Achieving simplicity isn't a simple matter. Mirabella sat in the corner drawing. Once she went out and came back with a six-pack of Old Milwaukee.

Studio time costs money, so an hour and a half later we began to pack up our instruments. Mirabella went round and showed her impromptu portraits to their original faces. They were fine sketches. Paul said, "We ought to put some of these drawings on our CD."

He turned to Mirabella and said, "Can I buy you a coffee?"

"Sure, why not?" She turned to us and held her hands up, fingers touching Namaste style. "Thank you for letting me listen to your music. Ciao, see you later," she said, blowing us all a kiss as she left with Paul.

Mirabella and Paul spent the rest of the afternoon smoking cigarettes in a small coffeehouse of the kind that doesn't exist anymore—a place where the tables and chairs didn't match and you could sit all day behind one espresso.

She took off her sunglasses and unpinned her black hair. While she spoke the whole intensity of her thin body was concentrated in her gaze. She didn't so much look at Paul as consume him with her eyes as she talked.

She had grown up in Buenos Aires and studied art in Mexico City. She had recently ended a bad marriage with a man who was in the art business. He helped her mount a show of her work in a known gallery. Almost half of the paintings in the show sold, but Mirabella never saw a peso of it. Her husband-partner-manager kept all the money and locked all his assets so that she had no access to anything but the apartment and car. After he did this, she wanted nothing to do with him anymore, couldn't even stand the thought that they lived in the same city, so she borrowed some money from her father and came to New York to stay with her gorda cousin.

She stood. "Now, with your permission, I will go to the ladies' room and powder my nose."

She came back shortly, sniffling and dabbing her upper lip with a Kleenex.

Paul said, "Looks like you powdered the inside of your nose instead of the outside."

"Here," she said, handing Paul a tiny vial. "Coca."

Paul went to the men's room, and when he returned it was his turn to talk nonstop: about his lonely suburban childhood, his decision to study music in spite of the disapproval of his family and half his friends. He took out a student loan to go to a conservatory in Ohio, where he studied composing and arranging. But it wasn't easy. He struggled to come up with something cerebral and modernist enough to please his professors. Meanwhile, he was gigging with rock bands and jazz ensembles at weddings and birthday parties and enjoying it more and more.

Finally he decided that he wasn't a composer and would never be one, so he left the conservatory without completing a degree. His father, who had been the loudest to oppose his enrollment, was the loudest to condemn his departure.

He said to Mirabella, "I really want to succeed, you know? But there are so many distractions."

They walked through Tomkins Square Park, past the nodding heroin addicts, the homeless asleep on benches, old Ukrainians out for a stroll, Puerto Rican children shouting and running around. The way she glanced at him made the earth stand still (his words, not mine—please!). Never in his life had he experienced such a sultry look. He was used to meeting sophisticated women who peppered their conversation with sarcastic remarks. He'd met women as bouncy as cheerleaders even after years in New York. Mirabella, by contrast, exuded boredom and languor—except when she was frantic.

As they walked nowhere in particular, he suddenly realized that he was on the cusp of closeness—he could take this woman in his arms and kiss her, which he did. Mirabella gasped. For a brief moment, she was flustered, but recovered her composure quickly.

"What do you want from me?" she said.

"I want to be alone with you. But I think my roommate's home now."

"My cousin works today. We can go there."

They went to her cousin's apartment, inhaled more coke and fell into bed. Paul was shy about giving details, but he told me that they didn't bother to get dressed for the rest of the weekend. When Mirabella's gorda cousin came home on Sunday night, she found two naked people foraging through the refrigerator. The cousin barked "Ladrones!" and went into her room and slammed the door shut.

"Did my bare ass frighten her?" asked Paul.

"No, it was the bare refrigerator. Most of the food is hers, she likes to eat a lot."

"Why didn't you tell me it was her food?"

Mirabella looked at him as if he were hopelessly stupid. "La pucha! We were hungry!"

Paul went up to the door of the cousin's room and shouted, "I didn't know I was eating your food! I'll pay you back! I'll buy new groceries! I promise!"

Mirabella pulled him away from the door.

"Don't worry about her, she is fine. Call up for some food to deliver. How about Chinese food? No pizza, please! The pizza in Buenos Aires is so good I cannot eat it here."

"Will you show me around Buenos Aires one day?" She kissed him on the cheek.

They ordered food and ate—still naked—with Mirabella's cousin, who by then had come out of her room. Paul got out his wallet and slipped her a twenty for the food when Mirabella wasn't looking. Then they showered, got dressed, and watched some TV. When Paul announced he was going to work, Mirabella asked if she could come along. Paul said, "Sure. Sit at the bar and we'll talk when it gets slow."

But the bar was crowded and he was so busy mixing drinks and settling checks that they hardly exchanged a word. Mirabella ordered mimosas till she was drunk. She left the bar without saying goodbye.

The next morning, at nine o'clock, the phone rang. Through a fog of sleep, Paul heard Joshua answer the phone. "Paul is still sleeping. He works the late shift at a bar—yes, yes, sure, I'll tell him. Oh, hi, Mirabella—qué tal?"

"I'll take the call," croaked Paul as he rolled out of bed.

He went into the kitchen and took the phone from Joshua.

"Paulie, querido, are you mad at me?"

"No. Are you mad at me?"

"No, for what?"

For a moment, confusion. Then they burst out laughing. "You left without saying goodbye…"

"I couldn't speak to you unless I ordered a drink…"

"Never mind, it's over," said Paul. "Can we get together today?" He fought through an enormous yawn.

She said, "I would love to, but I have the laundry to do and I must call my family. You know, calling Argentina is very expensive so we arrange in advance. I have especial free number, so I call a public phone very close to the family. Maybe some other time, querido."

But she showed up in the bar at 1:30 in the morning. With coke. She seemed to have an endless supply.

Two weeks later, she called up crying.

"I have a big, big problem. There is a letter from the Migra, the Immigration. They want me to answer questions. When they find out that I am illegal in this country, they will deport me!"

"You have no visa? "

"It expired. Months ago." Her voice quivered.

"Is there anything I can do to help?"

"No…no…but thank you, eh?"

"I'll marry you. For the green card."

"Please, Paulie, this is too big for a favor. Marriage is something… sacred."

"Not to me, it's not. It's just a bureaucratic label. And once you get your green card, if you think we're not sacred enough to stay married, we can get divorced. Divorce is another bureaucratic label."

"But…I can't pay you much. I don't have much money."

"You don't have to pay me anything."

"Are you joking?"

"No joke. I'll marry you if you need the papers."

She shrieked with joy. "Oh Paulie! Te amo—te amo—te amo!"

"I love you, too!" he said cheerfully. The words just popped out of his mouth. He had no idea if they were true.

When he told Joshua about the call, Joshua immediately asked, "When did that letter from the INS arrive?"

"I don't know, she didn't say."

"She could have gotten this letter months ago. You're just part of her master plan."

"Yeah? Maybe. So what?"

"Just be careful. Be really careful. You know, love is a sexually transmitted disease."

Paul said, "Did you get that from a Chinese fortune cookie? That's not my idea of romance, big guy. You are just wrong."

A week later I was on a subway going to City Hall with Joshua, Paul and Mirabella. The men wore ties and suits and the bride was in a classic little black dress. She looked so stunning, and Paul looked so nervous, that it was hard to remember that we were here only to placate the INS. We joined the line in front of the Civil Marriage Clerk's office. The variety of skin complexions, attire, and languages spoken did not hide a general mood of resignation to Fate. Mirabella whispered, "Maybe I am the only woman here who is not going to have a baby."

The ceremony took all of five minutes. A woman at a desk recited some legalese, the betrothed said "I do" and a document was stamped on both sides. They walked out of the office as husband and wife. I took pictures of everything for the INS. Mirabella seemed happy. She was giving Paul little hugs as we hopped a subway to Chinatown for a meal. Paul looked like a beach-stranded whale—out of his element, with uncomprehending eyes that blinked from time to time with astonishment. All his chatter about bureaucratic labels was gone. If getting married was a label, it was a label that could not be scratched off without damaging what it was stuck to.

A week later, when Joshua came back from his job at a printer's shop, he found a note on the kitchen table: Querido Paul I must meet some people for especial business. See you in 2 or 3 days my love so many besos.

The apartment was still. He listened for footsteps or other noise, but heard none. She was gone.

The next morning, Joshua was drinking cheap, strong Puerto Rican coffee and peering out the window at Tenth Street to see how people were dressed for the weather. He turned around to find Paul standing there in underwear, red-eyed and exhausted.

"What are you doing up at this hour, man? It's like 7:30."

Paul held up the note. "Did you see her today? Do you know anything about this?"

Joshua looked at it. "It was on the kitchen table when I got back from work."

"Can you remember if she said anything about where she was going? Or what kind of business she's in?"

"She deals coke. Didn't she tell you that?"

Paul almost took offense, but the conversation was too important to interrupt. "Not exactly. I guess she may sell it now and then."

"Come on, it's so obvious. How else do you support your habit when you're strung out?"

"Strung out? You think she's strung out?"

"Every waking moment, dude."

Paul was surprised. Mirabella liked to party and sometimes got carried away, but he had never thought of her as an addict. "Jesus fuckin' Christ! Strung out! What else didn't she tell me?"

Joshua said, "If there was a Nobel Prize for denial you'd be in Sweden, like, tomorrow, man."

"I'm going to call her cousin."

Paul picked up the phone and called the number Mirabella had given him. After some fifteen rings, La Gorda picked up the phone and began yelling, "Hey, cut out that ringing! Look, if I don' answer this hijo de puta phone by 5 or 6 rings, that means I'm busy or tryin' to sleep. Who is this?"

"It's Paul."

"Oh." A pause, then in a gentler tone: "Paul, I don't know where she went, she didn't tell me nothing, but she'll be back, you can count on it. By the way, congratulations on your wedding."

"Thanks."

"I pray you'll be together soon." She hung up.

"Fuck," said Paul. "Fuck fuck fuck fuck!"

"You need to expand your vocabulary," said Joshua. "I need to lie down. So if you'll excuse me..." Joshua grabbed him by the arm.

"What?" asked Paul.

Joshua said, "Don't let this chick get you strung out, too."

"I won't."

"You'll go down and drag the band down with you. Once you get addicted, your body doesn't want to stop, no matter how much it hurts. So don't start. Or I'll kick your butt."

"I hear what you're saying, Josh." But Paul's attention was far, far away. He slept through most of the day, got up, showered, ate a sandwich, played scales on his practice bass for a while, and went to the bar for the night shift. Each day felt longer and emptier than the one before.

But three nights later she was there when he got home from the bar. She was dressed in a conservative black pants suit with red high heels and a red crocodile-skin purse. She rushed to him and kissed him and hugged him.

When she realized he wasn't responding, she stepped back. "Something wrong?"

"Something is very wrong. You've been gone for three days! You could have at least called me once or twice so I know you're still alive."

"I left you a note! And I call! I call again and again, but nobody answer the fuckin' phone!"

"Are you sure about that? Joshua works during the day and I work at night, so there's almost always somebody here to pick up the phone."

"You don't believe me?"

Paul shrugged.

"Maybe I have the wrong number. Paulito, I love you. Do you believe me?"

Paul sighed and tried to master his annoyance. "Yes, but why do you disappear for days and hide things from me?"

"I do not want to hide anything from you, you are my husband now. But I want to protect you. It is better you don't know too much. If for you the details are necessary, I don't even start. But I tell you what I can, and it will be the truth, eh?"

Paul sat down at the kitchen table and lit a cigarette. "OK, tell me what you can."

"I sell drugs, OK? But I am careful. I dress always like a lady, not like some lowlife bitch. I never go straight to where I am going, but always go a different way every time. First I go to Jackson Heights to see some guys from Cali. They sell me the coca and I bring it to some people who live on Fifth Avenue across the street from Central Park. Is good quality, sells fast."

"God, that is so dangerous! You know what they'll do if they catch you? You'll never see daylight again."

"I can't make money legally here, so I must do illegal things."

"But if they catch you…"

"They are buying and selling drugs in the park here every day, and every hour of every day, and never the police do anything or arrest anybody."

"I don't want you to do this. It's too risky."

She gave him a hug. "When my green card comes, I will find a job, I promise you. OK?"

"Yeah, I'll believe that when I see it."

"The coca I got is very fine. Would you like to try it?"

"I don't want any."

"But I do." She opened her purse and began rummaging through it.

"I'm going to bed. Good night," he said, but she put a vial in front of him. He stayed awake.

The next afternoon, Mirabella did her nails while Paul practiced with an unplugged Fender bass. Joshua didn't show up. Later, as Paul was going through his closet looking for something clean to wear, Mirabella grabbed his wrist and shouted "No! Don't go to work!" Paul shook her hand off his wrist.

"Are you crazy?"

Mirabella said, "It breaks my heart to see you go to this stupid job of selling drinks to these idiotas. You should be home every day practicing your bass."

"Well, thank you for the thought," said Paul, "but I can't afford to stop working. And now that you're living here, Joshua's going to expect you to pay your share of the rent. "

"We have to find our own apartment—that's what married people do."

"Are we really married?"

"I have the paper that says we are. Do you think we are?" She wrapped her arms around him and pushed her face against his bare chest.

"Sometimes yes, sometimes no," he said. "It's all too new." He felt her nod her head. The intercom buzzed. Paul leaned over the messy kitchen counter and clicked on a white button at the bottom of the wall-mounted intercom. "Who is it?" For a moment, the sounds of cars going by in the street were audible over the intercom. Then a voice said "It's Joey."

"Joey! Come on up, man." The intercom crackled; the sound quality was poor.

"And walk six flights of stairs? I don't think so. I was just passing by and I wanted to tell you some good news for a change."

"What news?"

"We have a gig at the Gemini in Hoboken!"

"Hoo—hooray!" Paul jumped up and down and beat his chest. Joshua came to investigate. Paul told him that Joey Purple was on the lobby intercom.

Joshua leaned past Paul and pressed the white button. He heard the sound of street traffic. "Hi, Purple. This is Joshua speaking. How did you get us this gig?"

"The scheduled band had to cancel." Crackling. Static. "They're called Three Tall Twins. They were coming from Seattle by car and they ran out of gas and money in Michigan."

Joshua asked, "And the date is?"

"This Saturday night around ten."

Paul panicked. "We can't play on Saturday, we're not ready!"

Joey said through the crackle, "We'll never be ready to play in public until we start playing in public."

"I can't believe you said that. That's so fuckin' deep…Deep Purple."

Joey laughed. "Some delivery guy is down here and he needs to use the intercom. Peace and stuff." There was a click, then silence.

Paul went into his bedroom, where Mirabella was smoking cigarettes and leafing through an Italian fashion magazine, to announce that the band had a gig in Hoboken—on a Saturday night.

"Bravo!" she shouted and jumped out of bed to hug him. She whispered into his ear. "I would like to make a little party on Saturday afternoon."

"Not a good idea," Paul said.

"What time do you play?"

"Around ten o'clock at night."

She said, "I will invite friends for a cocktail hour maybe at two or three in the afternoon. You will have at least five hours to get to Hoboken. And you don't need five hours to get to Hoboken. Forty-five minutes maybe."

"You know what I really need? I need peace and quiet on the day of the gig,"

"Mi amor, it's just an hour."

"Let's do it on Sunday."

"But Sunday the music is over."

"No, no party."

"Let me have the telephone numbers of the grupo, please."

"They're all written on the wall next to the phone." He sighed.

Half an hour later she announced, to Paul's chagrin, that the rest of the band thought a cocktail hour in the afternoon was a terrific idea.

"I will organize everything. You go! Go! And practice with your fingers."

Paul called me on Saturday morning and asked to come over. When I opened the door for him, he didn't say anything. He was disheveled and morose. "Hey, what's happening? You look terrible but in a romantically hip way. Can you hold on to that mood till tonight?"

"It's not an act. I came here looking for some sympathy."

He sat down on the only chair I owned. One bed and one chair—that's all I could fit in the room I was renting. He withdrew a pack of cigarettes from a pocket of his jacket and gave one to me. He lit both cigarettes with a vintage Zippo lighter and we smoked in silence for a few minutes. He said, "I have to talk to someone about my problem, but it can't tell Joshua, because he's impatient with this kind of talk, and I can't tell my mother or sister cause they wouldn't understand." He coughed. "And I can't tell Mira, because she is the fuckin' problem. Can you keep a secret?"

"Whatever you say here will stay here."

"Thanks. The really dirty little secret is, Mirabella's addicted to cocaine."

I didn't have the heart to tell him that Mirabella's coke habit had become legendary throughout the East Village in a few short weeks.

Paul started to sob. "Man, I am so far from being able to convince her of anything—anything at all. No, it's worse than that. I can't convince myself about anything either. I decided to go on the wagon, but my willpower keeps failing and I end up doing line after line and then banging her all night long."

"That's not the part you want sympathy for, I hope."

"This is serious. I'm not denying that we love each other, but I just can't go near another little white line. It makes my hands unsteady, makes me babble, makes me sweat. I stopped going to the gym—a whole lot of other things. I'm afraid, man. I'm losing control."

"Tell her. Tell her what you're going through."

"That won't do any good."

"It's all you have to work with."

Paul stood and peered through the window to see a narrow strip of vegetables and greenery between two buildings. "Did you see this? Tomatoes."

"They're not ripe yet."

Paul said, "I'm not going to the cocktail party."

"You can't do that—this party is for you! She wouldn't do it for anybody else."

"But she'll pull out her vials and pretty soon I'll be all fucked up."

"Nobody is going to hold you down and force you to snort cocaine."

"But she weakens my resistance, don't you see?"

"Why don't you put in a short appearance?"

Paul moved to the door. "Maybe, maybe not."

"By the way," I said, "Joey called earlier. Did he call you?"

"Yeah. He said he rented a van."

"We're going to meet at six at the rehearsal studio and load up."

"I will definitely be there," he said as he went out the door.

"Come to the cocktail party!" I shouted as the door slammed.

He wasn't there when I arrived, but the rest of the band members were present, along with their friends and concubines. Mirabella had bought humus, pita, and falafels, still relatively new and exotic at that time. She had also made two dozen empanadas with cheese and ham and a Spanish potato tortilla and a big salad. On the kitchen counter there were some bottles of Argentine wine and a couple of bottles of harder liquor. It turned out that she had no actual knowledge of cocktails and couldn't mix one. We improvised. There were about fifteen people milling around. I chatted a little with Joey Purple's girlfriend, Suicide Sue. She spoke in a fixed monotone, never smiling, as if the lobes for facial and vocal expression had been surgically removed.

Mirabella flitted around the room with a mirror full of lines. I sampled some for medicinal purposes. The general chatter began to get louder, more nervous, more intense. It became really, really important to decide how much Richard Hell and the Voidoids owed to Iggy Pop and the Stooges. Some joints went around, but I didn't smoke anything.

Meanwhile, time was passing and still no Paul. Mirabella began to snort more and more coke. She went around the room inquiring about Paul. Finally the dreaded moment arrived.

Mirabella approached me and touched my chest with her finger. "Where is my husband?"

"I don't know."

She looked at me with a mixture of incredulity and rage. "You don't know?"

"He's not coming to the party," I confessed. "He's afraid he won't be able to resist the coke and he'll get too high to play tonight."

"That is ridiculous!"

"Look, I'm just repeating what he told me."

She sobbed. I tried to give her some napkins, but she refused. She went to the bedroom she shared with Paul and closed the door. When she emerged ten minutes later, all her makeup had been reapplied. She said," Now I'm sorry to say, the cocktail hour is over, you all gotta get out of here 'cause I don't want people say that I made the band late for the big gig!"

A murmur of rumors went through the crowd. Significant Glances were exchanged. By now everybody in the room knew that Mirabella's husband had not showed up. We all surrounded Mirabella and thanked her, and on the way out gave her heavy-duty Supportive hugs rather than light Social Event hugs.

The gig went fine. We didn't make many mistakes, the sound level was good, and we got a scattering of sincere applause after each song. Paul was clearly devastated by not seeing Mirabella in the audience, but he never dropped the beat. I thought I did good rhythm guitar work.

But somehow it lacked something essential. Call it soul, call it whatever you want, but if it's not there, the audience will fail to connect.

As we were packing our equipment, Mitabella walked in. The girl at the door said, "Ten bucks to enter plus one drink minimum per person per set."

"I'm with the band," said Mirabella.

"Which band is that? We have seven or eight bands here tonight. "I'm with all the fucking bands, bitch!"

Mirabella walked in with no further objections from the girl at the door; I turned to Josh and said, "Did you see that?"

He said, "Must be psychotic-ladies-get-in-free night." She found Paul. Her eyes flashed danger.

Paul said, "You missed the set. We just finished playing."

Mirabella retorted, "You missed the party!"

"I'm sorry, but it came down to a choice of furthering my career or becoming a babbling cocaine zombie. I chose my career."

"So that's what you think of me!" said Mirabella.

"No—no—Mira, that's not what I meant at all."

"But that's what you said!"

"Mira, I love you!"

"You got a funny way of showing it." She walked into the Gemini club and slammed the door behind her.

Paul turned to us and said, "Gimme a second. I just have to go in there and tell her something."

"No way, man," said Joshua. "You'll be in there forever. I just wanna go home."

Joey Purple said, "That's right. Either come with us or take your bass and your mike stand and get home some other way. But we're leaving in five minutes. I'm looking at my watch now to make sure it's five minutes and not six.

"Paul," I said, "she's bombed out of her mind. This is not the time to talk to her."

During the ride in the van back to Manhattan, Paul didn't say a word. There was some desultory conversation about the gig, but all in all it was a gloomy trip. The band broke up soon afterwards, but not due to rivalries or feuds or jealousy. Just lack of hope. To me, it felt like cashing out the few chips left over from a poker game I'd been losing all night.

I don't know if Paul and Mirabella ever spoke to each other again. I'm sure they did—her clothes and belongings were still in his apartment and she came back ten times to collect fifteen things—but Paul refused to say anything about Mirabella any more.

A few months later, on a wet, windblown and miserable evening. I got a call from Mirabella. She sounded panicky. "Please, I need your help! Right now! I am in a restaurant in Little Italy, and the guy I was with? He left the restaurant and never came back! Fuckin' bastard! And I have no money and the restaurant manager say to me he going to call the cops."

"So let him. You didn't steal anything."

"No! I cannot do that! No police! I can't explain that to you here and now, is a little complicated. But please—please come here and pay for the meal, and I pay you back tomorrow."

"It's really nasty and cold out," I said.

"I need your help!" It was more of a screech than a statement, and it resonated with anger and desperation enough to make me realize that I was afraid of this woman.

So I asked her for the address, got bundled up and headed for Little Italy. I entered the restaurant dripping wet and saw Mirabella sitting at a table alone staring off into space. It was an Italian-American family kind of place, small, expensive, with white tablecloths that a waiter cleared of bread crumbs with the edge of a small metal implement. There were practically no customers. She turned and saw me, but she looked exasperated rather than grateful.

"You take your time, eh? When I'm the prisoner of these Mafia guys here."

"I don't get it," I said to her. "Why didn't you cancel the order when this guy went missing?"

"I did cancel the order."

I waved the waiter over. He wore a green apron and black slacks. I said, "The lady says she canceled the order."

The waiter began to rub his hands together and said, "It was too late, sir. The food had already been processed."

"You can't make an exception? This was an unforeseen accident, not a scheme to steal anything from you. She hasn't eaten a bite."

The food has already been processed," said the waiter smoothly.

"The hell with it, give me the check and I'll take the two dinners to go."

"Very good sir." The waiter slithered off to complete these tasks. He returned with the check and two Styrofoam boxes. The check was crazy high, as I expected.

As we walked through the windy streets I asked Mirabella who had abandoned her at the restaurant. She mumbled, "A guy from a disco." Then she said, "Please don't tell Paul about this." I promised I wouldn't. She asked how he was, and I told her that he had given up the music scene and was now managing a catering business. She barely listened.

A little rain began to fall and I opened my umbrella, but it was difficult to keep it from getting blown inside out. Finally she said, "Could you lend me money for a taxi to home?" I gave her some money and one of the two Styrofoam boxes from the restaurant. She pecked my cheek and turned to hail a backwards in the street with her hand up. "I'm leaving New York in two weeks. I'm going to Buenos Aires. I'm going back to my husband."

"You mean your ex-husband," I said.

"No, no, no. My husband. Separated only, no divorce. I am still married in Argentina."

A cab pulled up. She climbed in and shouted, "I call you to pay back what I owe you!" The door slammed. The taxi accelerated and its back wheels sprayed me with rainwater.

When I got back to my apartment, I realized I was hungry. I opened the Styrofoam box and found one quarter of a stuffed artichoke, wilted and cold, maybe part of an appetizer. Nothing else.

My BFG

He sleeps on a couch in the living room. When he's not sleeping, he's watching TV. He goes to the kitchen to see if any food has magically appeared in the refrigerator since the previous commercial break. He doesn't seem to like the food that's in there. "What is this?" He holds up a flat square of yellow substance wrapped in a clear plastic.

"That's what they call American cheese."

"Put it out for the mice. It is better than a trap. They will die in agony."

He sighs and switches to a soccer game, but it is in Spanish and he doesn't understand a word. Once I tried to get him interested in baseball, but he fell asleep after 15 minutes. I don't know why. The game was a no-hitter. There's no excitement like watching one batter after another swing at the ball and miss it.

He sits up and says, "I will make dinner now. Get some chicken, lemon, garlic, onions, tomatoes and olive oil." He has to support both a XX-sized body and a taste for the fine cooking of his home in a remote Greek island.

"With what money?" I ask.

He shrugs. "Borrow some," he says.

It all started when I met Anna online. I was reading a blog about the Aegean Islands and she was looking for a recipe for stuffed grape leaves. We corresponded for a while. Then she flew to Athens, intending to spend the summer on a sleepy little island called Komatos. It was the sleepiest island in the Mediterranean.

For reasons that wouldn't make sense to anybody in contact with reality, I followed her. Yes, I found myself, just a few days later, disembarking from the local ferry boat and feeling sweat trickle down my back. I staggered onto the dock dragging my wheeled suitcase and blinking in the sunlight. The sea was dangling from the horizon like a rippling blue bed sheet. A bored fisherman was slapping an octopus against the stone piling of the dock to tenderize it. Sometimes he would leer at a tourist and offer to flog them in private. They didn't know that the octopus was a minor.

The island's only village consisted of one street and two shabby lanes that had given up all hope of being paved. I walked around for a minute of two, then decided I had had enough sightseeing. At that very moment, I ran into Anna.

"You're here?" I said. "Unbelievable!"

"Cut the crap! What are you doing here?"

"I…I…I just came for the sunshine. And to get some Greek culture."

"The only Greek culture left is in yoghurt. Why didn't you tell me you were coming here?"

"I tried to. I called, texted, tweeted, emailed, instant messaged, friended you on Facebook, Skyped, left a voicemail, sent an electronic greeting card, contacted you through What's App, asked you to join my LinkedIn network, Fed Ex'ed a letter, and posted a video of myself on YouTube and sent you the link."

"Oh, yeah, now I remember."

"You didn't respond in any way," I said,

"My lack of response was my response," she said." My silence had a subtext."

"My phone plan doesn't include subtexts."

She smiled. Maybe. It was hard to judge her mood because she never took off her sunglasses, even when she was wading in the sea. She was always trying to pass for a celebrity seeking anonymity. As long as she wore dark glasses, nobody could tell who she wasn't.

We decided to go the beach—it was only 20 centimeters from the town. But she barely noticed the beach, or me. Anna majored in lotion science at the Mono-Technical Institute of Cosmetic Studies and was now preparing to attend the upcoming International Ointment Biennale in Milano. When she wasn't on the phone discussing unguents, salves, and creams, she was reading about them.

We didn't talk a lot. "Now it is daylight savings time," she said, "but what I save each day, I squander each night."

"It's ironic that we get all our light during the day, when we need it least," I said.

"Do you have a nail clipper?"

I shook my head. Had the magic gone out of our estrangement? "When are you going to be nice to me?"

When Al Qaeda becomes a division of Disney."

"Well, there is some hope then," I said as I oiled up.

"Not for you. I'm having an affair with the keynote speaker of the Ointment Biennale. Dr. Han is a very wealthy man. He controls all the Tiger Balm in Southeast Asia."

"Don't rub it in."

"You're just jealous!"

"Of that grease ball? I don't think so."

We collected the towels and my little orange pail and shovel and walked up the path to the village where she had rented a large, shabby apartment. It was furnished with a few chairs and a faded lumpy sofa. Dr. Han probably stayed in penthouses or Swiss chalets. A goat was sitting in a corner munching on a copy of "Film Theory and Criticism." It ate only the reviews; the theory was too hard to digest.

My non-girlfriend began to pack her suitcase.

"Where are you going?" I asked. "Back to your Tiger Balm daddy?"

"Dr. Han is an influential man who can introduce me to many people."

"I know lots of people, too."

"Lots of nobodies. Dr. Han personally knows the man who wrote the Wikipedia entry on aloe vera."

"All by himself?"

"Once Dr. Han had sunburn and poison ivy. He applied both aloe vera and calamine lotion to the affected areas. He is a true pioneer. Excuse me, I must go."

She picked up the suitcase and walked out of the room, slamming the door in my utterly distraught face. Compared to this feeling, clinical depression seemed cheerful and despair was a party.

An extra-large Greek person knocked on the door and walked in. "I am owner of this house. How many more days you stay? Stay long as you like. Or even longer than you like. I accept all major credit cards." He rubbed his hands. "That woman went out from the island this morning. You let a sweet piece of baklava fall off your plate, my friend."

"Yeah, yeah."

"Don't be Mr. Sad Face. It happens to us all. Maybe more to you than to the rest of us, that is true. I have a story to tell you. Listen closely now."

"Do I have a choice?"

He cleared his throat and said, "I was in love with Maria, but she wasn't in love with me." He paused and smiled.

"And?"

He shrugged.

"That's your story? That's it?"

He stared at me. "Think of the wisdom it holds."

Three weeks later, I was still thinking. He knocked on the door and a bit apologetically handed me a bill.

I heard myself saying, "I left my checkbook in my desk in New York. Want to come up and have a cup of coffee while I write you a check?"

"In New York?"

He wanted to see the sights, visit Times Square, the Statue of Liberty, and see Broadway musicals, but I had never done those things before—no

New Yorker has, except when cornered by visiting relatives. My big fat Greek dragged me everywhere and paid for everything. Then he ran out of his money and began to spend mine. We became regulars at a belly dancing club. One night between displays of pelvic agility, I said, "What are we going to do when we hit the credit limit?"

My BFG said, "Apply for more credit."

"I just don't like the idea."

"Let's stop bickering and go out and try that new lobster place on the corner."

We went to the lobster place, caught a movie, tossed down ouzo and sang songs until the cows came home. The cows lived downstairs, and everything had to stop when they got home.

Today my big fat Greek was unhappy. "Look at this letter. They're going to deport me," he said, "I have no money left and no job. And I have too many debts back home. I could be in a dangerous situation. You know why Venus got her arms broken off? She owed money to the Milo mob."

He paced around. "Unless—unless we get married."

"No way!!"

"It's just for my status," he said. "I need a green card."

"But I'm not in love with you," I protested. "And I'm not gay!"

"Details" he said.

I said, "It's out of the question. Gay marriage is allowed. But in most states, marriage between two straight men is still a crime. Think about it. Who would clean?"

"Now we have perfect excuse to annul the marriage as soon as I get permanent visa."

"I don't know…"

"Good, it's settled," he said. "We'll have a big fat Greek wedding!"

I said, "How are we going to pay for a goddamn wedding?"

"Don't worry, leave it to me," he said. "We'll find some musicians to play for free. My mother will make stuffed grape leaves. We can borrow chairs from neighbors. My brother's wife knows a cheap baker. We can buy rings in monthly payments." He chattered on and on, I don't even remember half of what he said. In fact, everything from that point on is pretty much a blur.

But now I'm Mrs. Big Fat Greek. Would you like to try my moussaka?

Lost Shoe

Josef Dietrich was so shaken and enraged that he didn't notice that his shoe was missing until he was off the train. He was already loping along the platform when he became fully aware of a cold, nubbly feeling against the sole of his left foot. Looking down he saw a black sock where he expected a fine leather shoe to be. The remaining shoe looked quite forlorn. "I lost my shoe," he said, to his son Georgy who was grinning broadly, which meant he was absent, inaccessible. This was the last stop before the border. Hundreds of soldiers, mostly new conscripts, poured out of the train, forcing him and Georgy to keep moving.

Dietrich could have cried. It wasn't simply the terrible inconvenience, it was the loss of the shoe itself. He had his shoes specially made; he even had his shoe-trees carved to the precise measurements of his feet, so that his shoes would take on their shape and slip on perfectly. And he was no less careful with the rest of his wardrobe. He patronized the best tailors in Bucharest. If he happened to run into one his clients before or after a fitting, well, that was not the least advantage of dressing well.

Dietrich was, by profession, a notary. No business could be sold, no house could exchange hands, no financial arrangement of any significance could take effect without the notary's oath that all the details of the transaction conformed to the legal code. Many lawyers sought notary licenses but few passed the qualifying examination. Dietrich, however, was highly motivated. If he failed, his father would put him to work managing the family's kitchen supply business.

He was not only successful in law, but also in business. He found he had a talent for reconciling the opposing interests of competing firms. He was patient, stubborn, conciliatory and valued reason over emotion. As time went by, it became a standard rumor that "they're bringing Dietrich in" for this or that deal. Soon he had more clients than he could cope with.

When his father died, he sold the kitchen supplies to a cousin and bought a large house in the center of town, across the street from the French Embassy. A wrought-iron door wide enough to admit a motorcar or a carriage opened into a paved courtyard. One side of the courtyard was a building of flats that Dietrich rented out; the other side was a villa with his private residence on the top floors and the servants' quarters on the bottom floor.

He lived alone there, with only a housekeeper, a maid, and various handymen who came by as needed. But he spent most of his time in the office. When he wasn't in his office he liked to take tea in big hotels and entertain aristocratic ladies in private dining rooms where he could purchase the discretion of the staff.

Eventually, perhaps inevitably, he made a girl pregnant. She was from a good family, and was not grateful to be compromised by a casual affair. After a hasty, spiteful wedding, she took to her bed and avoided Dietrich in his own house until she gave birth to Georgy.

From the moment the baby was born, he was silent. He did not howl at birth, he did not cry in his crib, he did not laugh when somebody tickled him. He didn't utter a sound.

The mother was horrified, and regarded this affliction as her misfortune rather than the infant's. She returned to her parents' house and never came back. When Dietrich found out that she had left him with the baby, he was overwhelmed with emotions that he had never expected. He was relieved to be rid of the mother, and felt a deep, protective tenderness toward the infant, whose silence seemed to him a completely justifiable protest against the rising volume of urban noise. Dietrich dropped his social life almost overnight. He hired nurses to watch the baby, literally watch him, around the clock. Then he called upon every possible specialist in search of some explanation or diagnosis. Each one posited an entirely different cause for the boy's condition: malformed larynx…abnormal frontal lobe…traumatic separation. None of them held out any hope for a cure. Later on, Dietrich brought the child to specialists in bigger cities; the only difference was the fees.

It wasn't simply that the boy was mute. The problem was that he responded to the world only intermittently. Sometimes he was sensitive to the noises and colors around him, sometimes not. He didn't always understand what people were telling him, or perhaps he understood only in his own private way. He seemed impervious to all pressure to behave or conform, and only cooperated with others out of sheer generosity. However, his goodwill could evaporate if he were tired or upset. Then he became stubborn and unapproachable.

Interaction with other children was out of the question—he would spend hours rocking back and forth, uttering small sounds.

Although Dietrich worried about his son a great deal, his worries gradually became part of his routine. By himself, in his own context, Georgy was no trouble. His nanny could control him most of the time. In fact, Dietrich did not require much of the boy except that he not wipe his nose with his sleeve. Sometimes the boy came into his father's office and sat on one side of the great antique desk while Dietrich relaxed on the other side, glass of brandy in hand, talking about whatever crossed his mind, even the most obscure details of business law. Georgy's alertness and silence gave Dietrich the impression that the boy was listening to him, but he didn't understand the words. At night the lamp between them brought out the glow in Georgy's cheeks. Whenever it occurred to Dietrich that his little son would never be able to sit on his side of the desk, he shrugged the thought away. It didn't matter. His son would never want for money. He would see to that.

One day, a relative brought Dietrich's attention to a newspaper article about a nerve specialist in Paris who had developed miraculous techniques for giving the power of speech to the dumb—even in seemingly hopeless cases, like Georgy's. Suppressing some obscure misgivings, Dietrich composed a letter to the doctor—handwritten, not typed, for the matter was personal. Ten days later he received a reply advising him that he had a tentative appointment and they were awaiting his response. The appointment was six months away.

Instead of rejoicing at the news, Dietrich felt dizzy and had to sit down. A clamor of doubt and indecision filled his mind. Suppose this doctor could actually cure Georgy? A new Georgy, a speaking Georgy! Would that be an unmitigated improvement? Dietrich jumped out of the chair and paced the floor while he considered the matter from all angles. Though Georgy was afflicted, wasn't he comfortable? Content? Sheltered from harm? But if he learned how to talk, he would quickly become dissatisfied with his daily routine and no power could keep him from venturing out on his own. And he was unprepared and inexperienced, woefully vulnerable to the first bully or swindler to cross his path. He would be a target for anybody and everybody.

Almost trembling, Dietrich gripped his pen, and wrote back to the specialist, thanking him for his prompt reply and promising to set a date as soon his busy agenda permitted him to take leave of his business.

The person who had originally brought news of the miracle doctor to Dietrich's attention came to visit and of course asked Dietrich if he had secured an appointment. Dietrich mumbled that he hadn't gotten around to it yet. The visitor assumed an air of moral superiority. He told Dietrich that the doctor was extremely famous and busy, and that Dietrich had better act promptly, or else the doctor would keep him waiting for a long time.

The longer the better, Dietrich thought.

During the next few days, it seemed to Dietrich that half the town was busy telling the other half that he was an uncaring, negligent father. One after another, his family members found some pretext to meet with him, just so they could urge upon him this famous doctor, whom they knew nothing about. Though well-meaning, the family's concept of Georgy's best interests was so crude that Dietrich could find no way to reason with it. The only person who did not exhort or reproach him was Georgy's nanny.

Dietrich did not get angry. He listened politely to all the interferers and told them that the doctor's agenda was filled for an entire year ahead. A year later, most of Dietrich's acquaintances had forgotten the doctor completely, and those who did remember were confronted with Dietrich's considerable skill at verbal evasion. He kept them at distance with his rhetoric. He could do with words what his son did with silence.

At this time, Georgy was twelve. He amused himself with simple jigsaw puzzles and putting stamps from foreign countries in a book. On clement Sundays Dietrich accompanied him to the park and watched him push a model boat around the basin of a fountain with a long stick. There were often other boys playing around the fountain, sometimes roughly, but Georgy's nanny explained to them that they must not tease or push Georgy because he was different. So they left him alone, although they didn't refrain from making loud remarks about his handicap, as if he were deaf as well as dumb. And indeed, Georgy did not hear these remarks. Georgy could close his ears when he wanted to, just as easily and automatically as he could close his eyes. Dietrich had noticed this phenomenon many times. And was he willfully mute also? Had he decided to keep his mouth shut? Perhaps—but he could communicate when he needed to.

By means of a few economical and inventive gestures, he could indicate that he wanted to go to bathroom, or that he was looking for a particular toy, or that he wished to help the maid set the table for dinner. Sometimes, however, he rendered himself completely indecipherable, and responded to every entreaty with a broad, senseless grin.

But the boy's bad moods never lasted more than a few hours, and they were not frequent. In the midst of nerve-wracking business meetings, Dietrich would think about the money he was making for his son's future, and experience a calm swell of complacency.

Georgy's condition didn't get any worse as he grew up. He even found, now and then, some playmates among the meeker and milder children of the neighborhood, always much younger than him. But only temporarily. It was not his dumbness that drove them away but his intense solitude. When he grew tired of the game, he didn't become disruptive—that would only be exchanging one childish game for another. He just retreated into himself.

When Georgy was seventeen, his nanny got sick and died. The boy went through a long and severe episode of withdrawal. Dietrich was in anguish, also; he had depended on the nanny absolutely. He hired a new nanny but she complained that Georgy didn't want to have fun with her, that he was sullen, unfriendly.

She understood nothing.

Meanwhile, Dietrich's business was not going so well either. Of course it didn't help that he was always half-distracted with worry about his grieving son, but the biggest problems were occurring at a level far beyond his control. The political mood of the country, of the whole region, had become infected with fears and threats. Dietrich found himself accompanying his clients more and more often to the Ministry of the Army, until a colonel clapped him on the shoulder and said, "No need to see you again, Mr. Dietrich. We're not haggling anymore. From now on, we set the price and no supplier can legally refuse it."

War, thought Dietrich, as he shook the colonel's hand. War was coming. That was only one possible explanation for this new state of affairs. Dietrich reassessed his whole situation. War was coming, he was aging, and if worse came to worst, Georgy would have to fend for himself. And who would pay any attention to his small silence in the midst of a great uproar?

Dietrich sat down and wrote an urgent letter to the nerve specialist, the worker of miracles, not knowing if he still practiced at the same address, or practiced at all. But he did, and replied promptly. The doctor had decided to see him as soon as possible—in two months' time. Obviously he believed that international borders were in danger of closing. "We're going to take a long trip together. We're going to see a doctor about fixing your vocal cords. You want to speak, don't you?"

Georgy nodded his head slowly. In his gaze, apprehension and trust came together into one single, unanswerable question.

"We don't know if this will work. We're just going to go and see." Dietrich wrote to a hotel near the doctor's clinic and requested a two-week reservation. Might as well try to make a little vacation out of their visit and see Paris. It was also a chance to be fitted by some tailors and shoemakers whose new styles always arrived in the country a good year after debuting in France. All in all, it would probably be the last opportunity for leisurely travel for some time to come.

But when the day of their journey came around, and they stepped out of a taxi at the central train station, it became immediately apparent that the last opportunity for leisurely travel had already passed them by. The once orderly station was filled with soldiers who made a clamor that filled the interior of th building, echoing in the highest reaches of the vaulted ceiling. When Dietrich and Georgy finally got to their assigned train compartment, the conductor refused to honor their tickets. All first-class accommodations had been commandeered by officers; civilian ticket holders had to travel second class. Indignant, Dietrich dragged Georgy through crowds of khaki-clad young men shouting goodbye to family members, embracing girlfriends, weeping. The stationmaster sat besieged in his cage, surrounded by a terrible din. When he spied Dietrich, he bellowed, "You civilian there, you take whatever seat you can get!" His remark was followed by a burst of derision from patriotic draftees who had come to beg for standing room on the train.

Dietrich made his way back to the train, with Georgy following close behind, toting both their valises. He discreetly bribed a conductor, who quickly made room for them by forcing a couple of soldiers to give up their seats. Even so, the compartment was overcrowded and uncomfortable. They might as well have been in third class.

Finally the train began to lurch, and the discomfort was mitigated some-what by the idea that they were going somewhere at last. The soldiers who had lost their seats pouted with bored resentment. One of them pulled a flask out of his pocket and waved it around, provoking laughter from the crowded compartment. Georgy leaned forward and peered out the window as the city diminished from factories to sheds to isolated huts where goats grazed on weeds. The flask circulated around the compartment, accompanied by boisterous comments.

One of the standing soldiers said to Dietrich, "So, you bought a ticket for this train?"

"Yes I did," replied Dietrich. "For first class."

"If you join the army, you can ride for free!"

Dietrich shrugged.

Another standing soldier said, "If you bought a ticket for first class, how come you're riding here with us?"

"You asshole," said the first soldier. "First class is for officers and military jerk-offs. Civilians can't ride first class anymore."

"Why the hell should they?" cried another. "As long as we're defending them, let them eat some shit, too, and travel like we do!"

"I never said it was unfair," said Dietrich coolly.

"What did you say?" asked another soldier sitting across from them.

"Me? I said nothing," said Dietrich.

"Like hell," said the first soldier, accepting the flask. "Christ, it's empty!" He threw it on the floor and looked Dietrich in the eye. "Got anything to drink?"

"No."

"You going to report us for drinking? You going to tell the captain what we're doing? Tell him I think the officers in this army aren't worth a sick pig's fart."

"I'm not telling anybody anything. I was in the army myself once." This was a lie, but Dietrich thought he could pull it off.

"Oh yeah? Where did you serve?"

"Oh, here and there. Where are you going to serve?"

"Oh, me? I'm in the…"

Another soldier clapped his hand over the first one's mouth. "You're not supposed to tell anybody about your assignment, remember?"

"Look, I don't want to hear anything I'm not supposed to," said Dietrich quickly. "I just don't want to hear about it."

The train rattled along at a steady, lulling pace. Half of the soldiers lit up cigarettes; despite the open window, the compartment became smoky. The sun was declining. In a couple of hours they would reach Arad, where Dietrich and Georgy would change for a train to Budapest, where they would change for the Orient Express to Paris.

Dietrich stared at the fields going by, noting the progressive deterioration of the outskirts of the city, then the fields going by, a vineyard or two, then the farms, catching glimpses of men forging horse shoes and women carrying pails of milk, as if nothing had changed since the eighteenth century. At every local stop, no matter how small the station was, he saw one or two families of gypsies dressed in rags, unhealthy looking, begging for few coins.

After an hour had passed, the first soldier suddenly said to Georgy, "How come you're not in the army?"

Dietrich said to the soldier, "My son has a medical exemption. He can't speak. Do you understand that? He's mute."

"What a faker! Come on, he can speak!" Everybody laughed.

"He's completely mute, and I have documentation to prove it."

"Is that so? Well, you can wipe my behind with your documentation." A bigger laugh. Encouraged, the first soldier continued. "I can prove, without any documentation, that he can speak." He leaned over and put his face in Georgy's face. "You're just trying to get out of the army, aren't you? Isn't that so?"

Georgy's face went blank. The light in his eyes went out. "Leave him alone," said Dietrich quietly.

Ignoring Dietrich, the soldier said to Georgy, "Say something, anything, so I don't have to drag it out of you."

"Stop it. The boy didn't do anything to you."

"Oh yeah? Well, he's sitting in my seat!"

Dietrich rose. "You can have my seat if you want. Will that make you happy?"

"I want his seat, not yours."

"Hey!" said another soldier. "You hear what he said? He's offering you a seat! Sit on it and shut up!"

"So you're giving the orders in this compartment? What are you—a major general?"

"It's not a order, it's a fucking warning!"

A serious murmur arose from the rest of the soldiers. The two men continued to glare at each other until some other soldiers interposed themselves and physically separated the antagonists. The compartment sighed with relief and a few quiet conversations resumed. Outside, the sun touched the horizon and the reddened sky cast long shadows over a wide expanse of farmland.

Meanwhile, the soldier who had taunted Georgy continued to brood. Perhaps the present situation had touched some sore spot in his pride, or perhaps he was just a human landmine triggered to explode at the slightest pressure. In any case, the explosion came at an unexpected moment and caught everybody by surprise. Uttering a wordless jungle grunt, the soldier grabbed Georgy by the lapels, pulled him off the seat and pushed him as hard as he could against the other standing men, unbalancing them. It all happened in a few seconds. An indignant hubbub arose, but the soldier's voice was louder. "Say something, you little bastard! You faker!" Half a dozen hands gripped the enraged man, but the fury in him was so great that he managed to pull them down in a heap. Dietrich threw himself forward to protect his son but was immediately seized and pulled back. He and Georgy were ejected into the crowded corridor, disheveled and panting. Georgy tumbled to the floor, falling on his elbows. When his father tried to help him up, he pushed him away.

"Are you all right, are you all right," said Dietrich over and over between gulps of breath, but Georgy didn't reply; he only stood up and gave a odd grin. His eyes were dull and vague. "The valises," said Dietrich, still heaving with emotion. He pounded on the closed door of the compartment. No answer. He pounded again. Still no answer. A couple of soldiers in the corridor joined him, rapping on the compartment door until it opened a crack.

"My valises on the luggage rack," yelled Dietrich. "Two of them!"

The valises were passed into the corridor and the door shut again. The train plunged into darkness for five minutes and emerged in the railroad yard of the city of Arad, last stop before the Hungarian border. The soldiers were already pressing toward the doors.

A few minutes later Dietrich was on platform, and there he discovered that his shoe was missing. He didn't know if it had fallen off during the scuffle in the compartment or tumbled onto the track while he was getting off the train. Hoping against hope he tried to return to the train, but the crush of soldiers pushed him in the opposite direction.

"I lost my shoe," he gasped to Georgy, but Georgy didn't even look down, didn't even seem to realize that people on the platform were staring at Dietrich's stocking foot with amusement and interest, pointing out to one another the spectacle of an impeccably dressed man wearing only one shoe. It was impossible to conceal. Dietrich spotted a bench and rushed over to it. He sat down on the bench, put the valises side by side on the ground, and hid his unshod foot between them. Don't panic, he told himself. Of course—such is the law of bad luck—this was the first time he had ever traveled with only one pair of shoes. He had planned to order several pairs of new shoes as soon as they arrived at their destination. He remembered how he had hesitated in front of his closet before deciding not to pack an extra pair of shoes. Don't panic.

He reached into the inner pocket of his wool suit coat and took out his ticket and examined it. Fortunately, he had four hours to wait for his connection to the west. That gave him plenty of time to run into town and buy a pair of shoes. But he had to hurry. It was almost dark and the shops would close soon. He turned to Georgy and said, "I have to buy some new shoes. Look at me, I have only one shoe."

Georgy continued to smile.

"Stop grinning at me like that!" shouted Dietrich, and slapped Georgy's face. He had never done that before. Georgy looked shocked, confused. But there was no time for apologies and explanations. Dietrich lead his son to the main hall of the train station, where huge windows lit the interior like a cathedral.

"You stay here with the bags. I'll be back soon."

No flicker of response.

"I'll be back, alright? Soon, all right? Stay here until I come back."

It was obviously not a good moment to leave Georgy alone, but what else could he do? Travel all night and go through the customs of several countries with only one shoe? Border guards needed only the flimsiest excuse to turn people back, especially these days.

"I'm going now," said Dietrich. "I can't wait any longer, the shops are already closing. It's getting late."

Georgy began to rock back and forth as he used to do for hours when he was a child. It was a bad sign. Reluctantly, Dietrich hobbled along the platform till he came to a line of taxis. He approached the nearest taxi from behind, so the driver couldn't see his foot.

"I have to go to a shoe store. The nearest one, please."

The taxi took a few turns and stopped in front of a dirty, dim window. The street was full of run-down hotels and bars for commercial travelers. Dietrich paid and stepped out of the taxi, moving quickly behind the vehicle to keep himself more or less out of the driver's view.

He steeled himself for the inevitable jokes that would greet him when he walked into the shop, but he never got that far. Before he even got to the door, the window display stopped him cold. He had never, in all his life, ever seen a more hideous collection of shoes: pointed toes, ersatz gold monograms, boot-like heels. Impossible! He would look utterly ridiculous wearing a pair of these cheap and flashy monstrosities—like a street-corner Romeo.

He walked back to the curb, and as he did the unprotected sole of his left foot stepped painfully on a stone. His sock wouldn't hold out long against this kind of wear. He hailed a passing taxi. The taxi driver pointed out, with uncontrollable glee, that Dietrich was missing a shoe, and had probably left it behind in the shop. Gritting his teeth, Dietrich asked the driver to take him to a reputable shoe store. The driver frowned. He didn't know about such things; his wife bought his shoes for him.

Dietrich was furious. He got out of the cab and began walking. He asked everyone he passed where he could find a shoe store, and provoked a great deal of laughter. It was not only his stocking foot that attracted curiosity; he was also limping, and no doubt looked desperate and half crazy. Finally, he saw a shoe store.

It was closed.

He made a heroic effort to control himself, to resist the temptation to smash the window and grab some shoes and run. He approached the shop and looked at it more carefully. There was an apartment over the shop with all its lights on. He walked around and found a back door. He smelled cooking. After a moment of hesitation, he knocked loudly.

"Who is it?" shouted a voice from the upstairs.

"I need a pair of shoes! It's an emergency!"

"We're closed. Come back in the morning."

Dietrich pounded on the door again. "I need a pair of shoes right now! I lost one shoe and I have to take the train in a few hours!"

"I said the shop is closed!"

"I'll pay you double! I'll pay you anything! I've got to have a pair of shoes. I'm walking around on one shoe now and I have to catch a train soon!"

No reply. Dietrich thought he could hear a rapid conference between man and wife.

"Go to the front of the store, and we'll see."

"Thank you! Thank you! I'm going right now!"

Dietrich went back down the alley to the front of the store. He waited five minutes, ten minutes. He started to sweat with worry. Should he wait her longer, or did he still have time to go back to the other store and look for its proprietor? He cursed himself for not buying something in the shop near the railway station. Right now the idea of wearing two shoes of any kind, even the cheapest, vilest pair on earth, seemed like an unattainable fantasy. He turned around and realized that the eyes of the owner of the store were peering at him from a gap in the shutters. Dietrich opened his wallet and waved some bills.

"Size 40!" he said, stuffing bills into the gap

The eyes blinked and disappeared. The shutter creaked and rose just high enough to allow two shoes to be shoved underneath. Dietrich seized them greedily. "Thank you! Thank you!" The shutter slammed to the ground. Amazingly, the shoes were of good quality. Dietrich kicked away his single useless shoe and, kneeling on the pavement, put the new ones on. They fit badly, compared to his usual custom-made shoes, but they would do. He felt an enormous relief, as well as nervous exhaustion. He would sleep well on the train tonight, no matter how noisy or uncomfortable it was.

It took him a long time, almost twenty minutes, to find a taxi, but he arrived at the station with more than enough time to make his connection. Fortunately, most of the soldiers were gone. He went straight to the main waiting room. But Georgy wasn't there. Puzzled, Dietrich went into the station café and the men's toilet, but Georgy wasn't in either place. He couldn't begin to think where Georgy might have gone or why.

He went outside and walked the length of every platform, sometimes mistaking the back of somebody's head for Georgy's. Evening was displacing daylight. Everybody looked at him with hard eyes. Nobody smiled.

Dietrich walked around the main room again, looking at every single bench. He finally found the spot were he had left Georgy. His valises were on the bench, open and mostly empty. On the ground lay one of his white shirts, trampled by many feet.

Dietrich turned around and saw an old man in a tiny newspaper kiosk. "Did you see the young man who was sitting here? What happened to him? Do you know where he is?"

The old man made a gesture of dismissal. "In the army."

"My son isn't in the army."

"He is now. He was sitting right on that bench when the military police grabbed him and made him sign the oath. Then they took him away. It's the new law—didn't you hear about it? Everybody between seventeen and thirty has to join."

"But they can't do that! My son is exempt! He's mute! He can't talk!"

With a laugh, the old man said, "You don't have to talk to be a soldier. You just have to salute and get shot at. What can you expect? We're headed for bad times. Everybody is suspicious of his neighbor, and the government is suspicious of everybody. I know that war hasn't been declared, but peace hasn't been declared either." Noticing the look on Dietrich's face, old man turned away in embarrassment. Dietrich sat down and stared at his new shoes and tried to think nothing and feel nothing. He wanted to maintain his composure, at least for a while. Once he started weeping, he knew he would never stop.

Mount Olympus, NJ

She wore too much makeup, too much jewelry.

That was my first impression when she came into my office that cool March day to interview me between classes. I had completely forgotten about the appointment, was in a frenzy to finish correcting student papers that should have been handed back weeks before.

She was followed by a young woman with a professional video camera. This one was blonde, with a short, severe haircut, and an equipment bag slung over her shoulder. The camera's lens dipped down and looked me in the eye: a paralyzing intrusion. My first thought was that some catastrophe had occurred on campus, maybe even in the building. I braced myself for a shock.

"Hello, I'm Linda Bamarzo. I called you last week."

"Last week?"

"I'm making a documentary about orphans."

"Oh, right, right. Pleased to meet you."

A handshake and a whiff of perfume. "This is my assistant Brigit, she's from Germany. She's a film student who was orphaned at the age of nine. As for me, I might as well tell you that both my parents are alive and well. I just got interested in the subject of orphans because, well, I feel many of us with living parents just take it for granted."

I nodded wisely.

"I understand you're an orphan yourself," she said.

"No, I'm not an orphan, but my brother is."

She looked confused for a moment, then said, "That's a joke, right?"

I attempted a smile. "Excuse me, who gave you my name?"

She named another professor in my department. "Can I just ask you a few quick questions?"

"In front of that camera?"

"Of course, what did you think?"

"Sorry, I didn't realize you actually wanted to interview me about myself!"

"About who then? The fuckin' man in the moon?

"I thought it had something to do with mythology. That's what I teach, mostly. Although offhand I can't think of any myths about orphans. Romulus and Remus."

"You mean you made me come all the way here for nothing? You know how much this costs me? Every day that I spend on this project is another day of lost income for me."

"Sorry, I didn't think about that."

"And you're supposed to be teaching people how to think?"

I should have taken offense at that comment, but she seemed genuinely upset. I didn't say anything. She pulled out a handkerchief and dabbed at her eyes. Her assistant took a step back and pointed her video camera at us, but we both instinctively held up our hands to block the lens. However, she didn't turn it off.

"My mascara's falling apart. I use that kind that clumps up," she sniffled. "Is there a ladies' room near here?"

"Just down the hall," I said. "Look, I'm really sorry about this." And I invited them both to dinner at the Faculty Club. It was an invitation I was obliged to honor, because Brigit got it on tape.

Linda showed up alone, in an outfit far too fancy for the place, but it was not clear whether this was a mistake or not.

"Sorry I was so emotional the other day, but it's hard to see your work not succeeding."

"Pretty awful," he said.

"I would think so."

"Where's Brigit?"

"Busy," she said.

I was disappointed, for Brigit had seemed the more interesting of the two. Linda called for a menu and began to discuss every entreé in detail, asking me a lot of questions and laughing loudly at the slightest pretext. She was wearing an ornate gold necklace with tiny little diamonds in it. She looked like a real-estate developer's mistress.

She must have noticed me assessing her appearance. She began to look around at the other women in the place. "Who are those bag ladies at that table?" she said in a whisper that rocked the room.

"I believe those bag ladies are the wives of the engineering department," I said.

"Those frumps probably have a lot of money," she said. "You can tell by the way they dress. Reverse snobbery."

"Tell me, what inspired you to make a documentary about orphans?"

"It has to do with a car accident. I went through a Plexiglas window face first. But I don't want to think about it. Let's have some more wine."

Her conversation was banal but lively, which loosened me up considerably. No need to make any big efforts to impress her. Quite the contrary. I was sure that she would regard any attempts at urbane discourse as Faculty Club snobbery.

At the end of the meal we went out in the parking lot and shook hands, and that should have been the end of it, but we stood there talking about nothing in particular for at least an hour. People emerged from the Faculty Club in twos and threes, got in their cars, and slowly drove past us. Finally Linda said, "I must be completely crazy, but why don't you follow me in my car back to my place."

"Look, are you sure about this?"

"Are you coming or what?"

She took off at high speed. It was all I could do to keep up with her. Her apartment was the first floor of a small house. It was an unlikely combination of feminine hideaway and video equipment warehouse. The carpets were fluffy, the curtains sumptuous, but the center of the living room was dominated by a giant TV hooked up to an editing deck by a medusa-like tangle of cables. There were piles of videocassettes under the glass coffee table.

"You know what my trouble is?" she said. "I've spent all my money on this damn documentary and it still isn't going anywhere."

"These things take time," I said.

We started to get very comfortable together on the couch. I was trying to go slowly and not apply any force, but there wasn't any resistance at all. We melted and dissolved like sugar in the rain. Then she lead me to her bedroom and that's where I woke up alone the next morning. She had been up for some hours, and she already had too much makeup on.

"I always jump into bed with men and it never goes anywhere," she said. "I enjoy it for a moment and then it all gets ruined somehow." She began to wipe her eyes with the back of her hand.

"I have to go. I have to teach today."

She pulled me to her and hugged me. "Call me, OK?" I did call her. In fact, I invited her over for dinner.

Did I mention she was beautiful? Did I say that I was lonely?

I was working on a scholarly article about the history of the Muses. But it wasn't going well at all. I was frustrated and it seemed like a good idea to get away from my desk for a while and come back to it later. It seemed like a practical thing to do. Of course, what often appears to be practical at the moment can be highly impractical in the long run.

For dinner I made steaming moussaka with rice, using all the cooking utensils that my wife had chosen so carefully a long time ago. Now she was eating out of somebody else's dishes and I was stuck with hers. They were too expensive to throw out for merely sentimental reasons. Linda brought a bottle of wine and ate like three people.

After dinner I put my favorite music on the stereo. Her reaction to baroque and bebop alike was the same: "Wow, that's really different!" If she had been one of my academic friends, I might have discussed the music with her, but she was not interested in discussing anything, it seemed, but my lack of parents.

I had lost my parents far too late in my life to be able to claim any special status or psychological condition, except grief, as a result of their rather timely demise. Her parents, it turned out, were divorced. She didn't seem too eager to talk about that. When the conversation lagged, I kissed her. She kissed me back, and there seemed to be no particular reason to stop until we were in the bedroom. She took everything out of me and turned it into gold.

When we were finished she went to the bathroom to repair her lipstick. I was a warm, muddled heap of bliss. Despite my feeble attempts to coax her back into bed, she went into the kitchen and washed the dishes. She came back to the bedroom long enough to get dressed and announce that she was going home. I was a little hurt but she warned me not to argue about it.

So we began seeing each other, going out together, hooking up, whatever it's called. I don't really know what she saw in me. I can barely say what I saw in her—I mean if I looked below the surface. But what a surface! I loved displaying a good-looking woman on my arm, not to impress strangers on the street, but for the sheer adolescent fantasy of it.

Sometimes rude reality intruded. The few times we ran into people I knew, I found her loud, brassy manner embarrassing. She had no qualms about shoving her documentary into any kind of conversation. Every person she met was a potential audience member for a film that wasn't even half done. I thought the whole project was doomed from the start, but I didn't say so. Instead I told her that any medium more recent than papyrus was outside of my field of interest. So we never discussed it. And of course we certainly didn't discuss my scholarly work. Nor did we talk about the future, the past, or anything that might suggest that we had a relationship at all. We filled up the air between us with inconsequential matters, like what we were doing tonight or tomorrow night and whether we should go out for dinner and whose car we should take. The most serious question she ever asked me, I think, concerned my religious beliefs. I told her that, in my considered opinion, the earth was just a battleground for the gods. She frowned and said, "What good does believing in that do you?"

Though she refrained from discussing her documentary with me, Linda did complain about the financial problems that it was causing her. We would hardly have gone out anywhere if I hadn't insisted on paying for both of us, usually over her objections. I didn't mind. I even offered to take her with me to Greece to me in the early summer. She tried to laugh off the whole idea. "Greece? You must be kidding! I can't even afford to take the train to New York. I'd have to get off in Newark and walk the rest of the way."

"The plane tickets are on me. And we don't have to pay for hotel rooms. I have friends in Athens."

"What about my film?"

"Just put it aside for two weeks." She kissed my forehead.

Of all the things that annoyed me about Linda, nothing bothered me quite as much as her habit of deserting me in the morning. If we were at my apartment, she'd be gone before I opened my eyes. If we'd spent the night at her apartment, she'd get up first and lock herself in the bathroom for a good hour. I complained about it, I joked about it, but nothing could dislodge her from the bathroom before she was good and ready to leave.

One morning I even went outdoors to piss, a pleasant enough way to begin the day if you're camping in the Canadian Rockies, but much less so in suburban Jersey between a garage and a fence. I zipped up, went back inside, and pounded on the bathroom door.

"Open the door, please."

"I'm not ready yet!" she yelled through the door.

"That's the whole idea! I want to see you not ready!"

"What?" A long pause. "I'm afraid that's impossible."

"Why?"

"I just told you, I'm not ready. And the more you keep shouting at me, the longer it'll take me to get ready."

"I want to see you without your makeup."

"What for? Just to see how plain and ugly I really am?"

"No, to see how beautiful you really are."

"Yeah, right."

I left before she came out of the bathroom. That afternoon, she didn't call, but I wasn't sure if she was angry or merely busy. I think she was researching grant possibilities and looking for more de-parented people to interview. I had a strong suspicion that Brigit was mostly filming Linda. The two of them would end up with a documentary about a failed attempt to make a documentary.

Two or three days passed in silence. When she finally called, I invited her over for dinner. I didn't bother to make anything special, and she didn't seem to expect it. I dragged my TV out of its usual hiding place in the hall closet and set it up on the coffee table so she could watch something or other. When the program was over, we sat together not speaking, just leaning against each other.

And I brought up the forbidden topic.

"Please let me see you without your makeup."

"No."

"Let me see," I repeated.

"Drop it."

"Look," I said, adopting my wise-and-patient-teacher tone of voice. "I think the human face was meant to be seen in its natural state. I happen to like women without makeup."

"Now you like women without makeup? So that means you don't like me?"

"Of course I like you—I'm very fond of you—very fond. You know that." I felt as if I were handling hazardous material without the benefit of safety gloves.

She said, "Alan, I like to wear makeup. Just accept me for what I am."

"But who are you? You won't let me see. You must always have some kind of mask on."

"I better be going," she said with exaggerated dignity. I didn't try to hold her back. Over the next few days, I hoped she would call, but she didn't. I found myself becoming very irritated with people who did call, as if they were perpetrating some cruel practical joke by summoning me to the phone and then not being Linda. I finally broke down and left a message on her machine. Then I left another. She called back and told me very brusquely that she was busy and didn't want to be distracted from her project anymore. I sensed something very hard and determined in her tone, an intransigence that lay beneath the vacillating exterior of her moods like rocks deep below a stormy sea.

Now that I was separated from her, I saw her better. Despite her frequent perturbations, she was a determined person. She would indeed finish her documentary. It might not be very good, but she would complete it and perhaps even find an audience for it.

I let her be for a month or more. Then, one sunny Friday afternoon after class, I impulsively picked up the phone in my office and called her. She seemed pleasantly surprised to hear from me. Rolling with the momentum, I asked her if I could drop by. There was a moment of hesitation before she agreed, and it hurt me. But I went to see her anyway.

Brigit answered the door. Linda was sitting on the couch with a young man who wore a neatly-pressed shirt, new jeans, and designer glasses. They were watching a videotape of Linda interviewing him. "Oh, no, don't leave that in!" he said, and they erupted into noisy laughter. I lingered at the front door; I didn't want to intrude on this narcissistic moment.

Linda stopped the tape when she saw me.

"Oh, Alan, come in and join us. Don't just stand out there on the steps like a Jehovah's Witness. Come here, I want you to meet Charles. He's an orphan I found for my film. Alan is a professor at the university."

We shook hands.

"Are you an orphan, too?" he asked me casually, as if inquiring about my hobbies.

"Technically. My parents passed away when I was in my twenties, but they were already old."

"Well, Linda," Charles said, "looks like you're the only one here whose folks are still alive."

"For all the good it does me!" she exclaimed. "My father walked out on the family, then my mother and me we almost stopped talking to each other. We keep in touch, sort of, but I can't really have a conversation with her."

"You never told me that," I said.

"Yes, I did," she said, sniffing a little. "I think I did."

At that moment it occurred to me that she had never really talked about her parents in the present tense, as people who were part of her life. If I hadn't been parentless myself for so many years, I would have been quicker to notice this. I sat down and watched a videotape of Charles describing a Dickensian childhood of bouncing from one foster home to another. He was straightforward and unemotional; he let the story speak for itself. Every so often Linda gave him a look of pity and squeezed his hand. When it was over, I made some banal remark about his determination to survive and told Linda I had to be going. She came out to the porch with me. It was early spring, and the light seemed to loiter in the sky long after anybody could really use it. People were already home from work, and reluctant children were being summoned inside for dinner.

"So what do you think of the interview?" she said.

"It's good, it's very good."

"We really needed some material like that. It's going to help a lot."

"Excuse me for changing the subject," I said, "but what happened to us?"

"Biology happened," she snapped. "We were attracted to each other, that's all."

"No, I mean what happened to separate us?"

She didn't say anything.

"Look," I said, "I promise that I'll never bring up the subject of makeup again. I will never refer to facial cream, lipstick, rouge, mascara, or even soap."

She frowned. "You know, once guys get on my case about my makeup, they never let go of it, no matter what they promise. No matter if they think they're promising. I found that out the hard way."

I gave her a peck on the cheek and went to my car. In my rearview mirror, as I was pulling out of the driveway, I saw the front door shut. What was I expecting to see, anyway? Linda sobbing into a big white hankie?

For the rest of the semester, I threw myself into my work. Much to the dismay of my students, I developed a florid, hortatory style of lecturing, as if the survival of the classics in the West depended on their completion of the weekly reading assignments. Which may have been true in some sense, but what did they care? I handed out grades and repainted my kitchen. The only thing I couldn't do was finish my scholarly article about the Muses. I just couldn't remember what I wanted to say.

Finally the eve of my departure to Greece arrived. I took out my old backpack and threw in some summer clothes, a kit for toiletries, a notebook, a few books.

The next morning the sun was shining brightly and I was ready to go. But I had overlooked one detail. My plane didn't leave until ten at night. Then I got an idea—I would stop by Linda's place and say goodbye to her. It was late morning. She would have her makeup on by the time I got there.

She seemed glad to see me when she came to the door, but far from overjoyed. She invited me in and shoved two cups of stale coffee into the microwave, She looked nervous and pensive. Suddenly she began yelling. "What did I say or do to make you think that I ever wanted to see you again? Why do you keep crawling back? You shouldn't be here, it disrespects my feelings!"

I said, "I get the message. It's over."

She expelled a long sigh. "Finally! You're not a bad person, Alan, but you have a thick skull."

"It's over. It's over. It's over."

"I hope so. "

"You want to come to the beach with me for a couple of hours? I know that it's over but it would be a shame to waste such a beautiful day."

"I was thinking of the beach this morning. I need to get out of this room. But I'm afraid of sending you the wrong signal."

"It's over. It's over. It's over. Anyway, I'm going to Greece tonight and may move there permanently if I can find a teaching job."

She thought for a moment and said. "OK, let's go." She jumped out of her chair and left the room. When she came back she was wearing a big floppy straw hat, giant sunglasses, and a dangling straw bag. Her legs looked spectacular in shorts. "OK," she said, "I'm ready to hit the beach, let's go."

We drove in separate cars so we could go our separate ways afterwards.

It was a Friday, but traffic to the shore was not nearly as bad as usual. And the beach was not too terribly crowded. Fearful of the sun's power to scorch and wrinkle her fair skin, Linda insisted on sitting in the shadow cast by a hot dog stand, despite the odor of grease and the noise of banal pop music that emanated from it. We waded into the ocean. She wore her sunglasses because she didn't intend to go in deeper than her knees. The wind picked up and freakishly large wave unbalanced her and she fell into the water.

I grabbed her hand and pulled her up so she could regain her footing. At that moment, I realized that I was looking at her naked face. Almost all of her makeup had washed off. I had only a few seconds to look at her. I saw a lot of scar tissue on her cheeks and forehead, but it was far from disfiguring. It was the kind of scarring that dominates your first impression of someone, but disappears with familiarity. She was still beautiful. Beautiful with scars.

We sat down in the sand, more apart than together. She looked upset. She kept touching her face. She said, "It's nice day to be outdoors but I need to go home and get some work done." She squeezed my hand and stood up. "Good luck, professor." Then she left.

I lay there sweating, buffeted by the boisterous cries of bathers, the smell of fries, the steady lapping of the waves. I saw Mount Olympus was looming above me, far closer to Jersey than I would have guessed. Apollo and Dionysus were eating ice cream, satyrs and nymphs were splashing in the water. Children's voices shrieked with mindless excitement as I inhaled the pungent aroma of rotten kelp that was strewn over the crowded beach.

The Puppeteer

After she put away the paper, the glue, the finger paints, and the boxes of wooden sticks, taken down from the walls the scrawled paragraphs proudly bearing gold stars, sat through the graduation of the sixth-graders and had her picture taken innumerable times by parents and by kids—after all that fuss, the school year was over. Joan packed in a hurry, took her car to the garage to be tuned up, and left Boston by the Mass Pike to visit her recently divorced sister in Arizona. She wasn't going for her sister's sake, however, but for her own.

She had long had the feeling of floundering, of being at loose ends, and hoped that a few days of driving would be calming and distracting. And if that didn't work, Martha would be there at the end of the ride, ready to help Joan reconcile the alterations of her mood, from gnawing doubt to reckless overconfidence.

Divorce notwithstanding, Martha was steady one. Joan called her every night from another roadside motel and talked for an hour. "If you keep this up," said her sister, "we won't have anything to talk about when you get here. We won't have anything to do but eat nachos and watch soap operas."

"Oh yeah?" Joan couldn't tell if her sister was serious or not. "In curlers?"

By the time Joan got to the desert, she had decided that this road trip was forcing her to think too much, and thinking too much always lead to dwelling on the negative. Looking for some relief from her self-imposed solitude, she jabbed at the car radio, but all she could find was ranting pastors and screaming deejays.

She was bored. Otherwise, she would have never slowed down to look at the handsome hitchhiker. At an impulse, she stopped twenty yards past him and turned around to watch him as he scurried for the car. If he looked unacceptable at close range, she thought, she would hit the gas and take off. But he looked dusty and bedraggled He didn't look like a psychotic killer. He hauled a backpack and a large duffel bag in the hot sun.

"I hope you're not carrying body parts in that bag," said Joan.

"Not parts. The whole bodies," he said in a foreign accent as opened his duffel bag and drew out a large wooden puppet costumed in motley silk and a blue conical hat. Its expression was comically arrogant. "I present to you now Arlecchino." Joan's eyes darted between the highway and the puppet. The puppet bowed and said, "And I present to you now my master, Flavio Contina." The hitchhiker bowed. A rather false female voice, coming from somewhere else, said, "And I am Columbine. We all have the honor to ride in your car, and thank you for your trouble."

Flavio said he was on his way south to the border and then to Guadalajara, but didn't seem to have pressing business there or anywhere else. He eagerly accepted Joan's offer to have lunch at Martha's house. Joan's sister was surprised and displeased to find her reunion with her sister contaminated by the presence of a strange hitchhiker. It was an awkward moment for everybody.

Flavio tried to project an air of nonchalance, as if he were an unimportant bystander. But there was something colorful and vibrant about him that could not go unnoticed. Flavio's seemed like a lost cockatoo here on Martha's silent suburban street in the full blaze of afternoon, where rows of identical houses awaited nothing.

"I invited him for lunch. I hope that's OK," said Joan, whispering.

"What are you doing with this character?" said Martha harshly, not bothering to lower her voice.

"Doing? I'm not doing anything with him."

"This is crazy! Who the hell is he? He could be anybody!"

"It's great to see you again," said Joan, throwing her arms around her sister's neck.

After lunch, Flavio took Arlecchino out of his duffel bag and unwound the marionette's strings from a bobbin. The main control looked a little bit like a miniature coat rack—a wooden bar with protruding dowels, each attached to a control string. The top cross-bar, which controlled the legs, was detachable. He could take the cross-bar off its hook if he wanted to move the legs more independently, or he could leave it on the main tree and use his free hand to pluck at individual strings and produce more subtle effects, like lifting an eyelid or flicking a wrist

He made Arlecchino sing a song in Italian, and wave his wooden wand, and wink at Joan. For some reason, she was more powerfully affected by this puppet's randy eye than by any male gaze that had ever sought to provoke her. She had to repress a ridiculous impulse to slap the puppet's face.

"Gorgeous puppets," admitted Joan's sister. "Where did you get them?"

"I make," said Flavio. "They are mine." He looked at the two women as if they were abysmally ignorant. He seemed all at once to fold up, to collapse; fighting off yawns, he asked if he could lie down somewhere. Permission was quickly granted, for the two sisters were eager to get beyond the preliminary excitement of seeing one another and rebuild their intimacy. But it wasn't so easy. Their relationship was not balanced. It never had been. Martha tended to deliver fully-formed opinions, one after another. She might listen to criticism, but only after her original idea had been completely formed, and not a moment before.

Joan, on the other hand, swam in a flux of speculations and surmises. She couldn't make decisions; she saw all the alternatives, all the roads not taken. She always had a lot more to talk about than her sister did; however, the more she talked, the more the answers seemed to elude her, to change shape and direction. Thus her teaching career, her friendships, everything she did was compromised by uncertainly and hesitation.

Martha decided that Flavio wasn't dangerous and could sleep on the living room couch if he wanted. He seemed grateful for the respite from hitchhiking. The three of them drove out to the desert to watch the sunrise. In the afternoon they drove to the local tape rental place and collected some movies.

The third day of her visit, Joan thought she heard her sister sobbing in the bathroom. She tapped on the door.

"I'm in here!"

"Marth, it's me. Open the door!"

Martha opened the door. Joan hugged her and said. "What's wrong? What on earth happened?"

"My ex…I just talked to my ex."

"What did he say?"

"Who cares? I married an insane person! It's over. He's history."

Martha suddenly broke the hug and looked around self-consciously. "Where's the guy?"

"Flavio is in the kitchen. He's making lunch." Then she hugged Joan even more tightly.

A few hours later, in the kitchen, Martha said, "Mind if I…?" She gestured in the direction of the living room, where Flavio was watching TV.

Joan shrugged. "Why should I mind?"

"Are you sure? Absolutely sure?"

"Knock yourself out," said Joan. That night, she woke up in inexplicable agitation. As she shuffled to the bathroom, she heard noise from her sister's room and noticed that her door was partly open.

She approached and saw the pale gleam of Flavio's back in the darkness.

One of her sister's shapely legs dangled out of the sheets and flexed with involuntary reactions. Joan had never seen her sister in bed with anybody before, and found herself more critical than anything else. Martha wasn't letting herself go, she wasn't really open to the experience.

But as Joan silently deplored her sister's lack of sensitivity, she began to feel an alarming sensation of guilt. She quickly went to the bathroom and took a sleeping pill.

The next morning, when Flavio was in the shower, Joan touched Martha's

79

arm and said, "You know, I think I made a mistake yesterday. I think I do mind."

"That's OK with me. I'm finished with him." She made a flinging gesture. "Just felt like pulling the puppeteer's strings, know what I mean?" When Joan didn't reply, her sister added, with irritation, "For chrissake, it was nothing!"

After breakfast, Flavio mixed some tequila with orange juice. Flavio embarked on a day of glorious intoxication. He made Columbine dance the can-can and sing "Stayin' Alive" and other songs unlikely to be part of the repertoire of an eighteenth-century style puppet, all in a heavy Italian accent. He started smoking cigarettes; when Martha objected, he dismissed her indignantly—she simply didn't understand men's needs. He insisted that Joan take up Arlecchino's handles and he took Columbine's. Even drunk, or especially drunk, Columbine could pirouette with a saucy grace.

Next to her, Arlecchino moved clumsily, hesitatingly. But Joan loved the feel of the wooden controls in her hands. Her body passed its motion into Arlecchino's, and for those few moments when by chance she managed to make the wires obey her intentions, she was Arlecchino.

Next morning, as Flavio slept off his binge on the living room couch, Martha told Joan that she had taken enough days off from work. It was time to put on nails and eyebrows and get back to the job. Although she felt a twinge of abandonment, Joan loved Martha in that moment. Her bluntness clarified the world, cut through its crap.

Flavio awoke around noon, complaining thickly about the chill of the air conditioning. His face was gray and drawn, devoid of the fierce capriciousness that had animated him the previous day, but coffee and aspirin brought him part of the way back to life. He sat the marionettes on the couch and made Joan touch each wire on each body and follow its path to the main control. Afterwards, he gave her a lesson in manipulating Arlecchino.

When Martha came home from work she invited them out to a chic California style restaurant. Flavio tried to refuse; he was on a tight budget and couldn't afford to pay for his own meal, let alone anybody else's.

But Martha insisted on treating everybody. During the meal, Martha and Joan sat on one side of the table and Flavio on the other. The sisters teased him about being the unemployed father of two wooden children. Flavio responded weakly, unconfidently. They teased him about that, too. He bowed his head and picked at his elegant arrangement of tuna and arugula with little appetite. But at the very end of dinner, he inexplicably recovered recover his usual good spirits. His large, dark eyes brightened. He seemed to emerge out of darkness, like a sunrise.

Martha went to bed early. Flavio and Joan remained together at the kitchen table drinking and talking quietly. The silence and dryness of the air outside transmitted the distant rumbling of semi-trucks and the faint swishing sound of passing cars. Joan didn't enjoy alcohol very much but she loved to drink— which meant, to her, sitting like this and immersing herself in whatever the moment had to offer, the company of others, the mood of a particular place, or the drift of her own reverie.

Flavio reached over the table and took her hand in his. He squeezed her hand, kissed it. "Listen to me," he said. "You joke that I am a father, but is true, is true—these puppets are my children. But I cannot manipulate both. I need help."

"What do you mean?" Joan felt as if she were about to faint, not from losing consciousness, but from losing control.

"I need two more hands."

"But I don't know anything about puppets."

"Yes you do. Arlecchino wants you."

"Oh, please."

"Arlecchino needs your hands."

When Joan couldn't bear it any longer, she lead Flavio upstairs to her room. As they embraced, he murmured something about Colombine. She felt a tremor of jealousy. Then realizing how insane that notion was, she said, "Shh, don't talk anymore."

They went south together, crossing the border at El Paso, driving straight through the night on the bumpy road that brought them into the heart of Mexico, past mountains silvered by moonlight and slopes of spiked yucca.

In Guadalajara, they slept on the floor of a Mexican puppet maker's studio. They woke up in the morning surrounded by shelves full of puppets displaying every conceivable emotion, from contentment to fear to triumph to sadness, a tumult of feeling that alarmed Joan. Flavio showed no sign that Joan's presence changed his life in any way.

And maybe it hadn't. He had been on and off the road, both in Europe and the United States, for a year or two, living on odd jobs here and there and shacking up with God knows who or what. So perhaps he had had enough romance already. He behaved as if they were already deep into a long-established marriage. He took her for granted, as if they had already confided in each other for a long time. It was the best of both worlds—an intimacy that did not pick scabs or probe wounds.

They turned the car from Guadalajara to the coast, to a small village not far from the ocean. They stayed in a room that faced a courtyard with a small dry fountain and a dusty tree. The concrete floor of the courtyard was also the floor of the surrounding rooms, and the mattress they slept on felt like a bas-relief map of Mexico itself. The mountains stuck in her shoulder blades when they made love. The room's only window gave on to the courtyard, and had no glass—only a crooked wooden shutter that Flavio threw open to get some air. Anybody passing through the courtyard could have glanced in and seen their private life—Flavio sprawled out naked with a bottle of tequila, Joan huddled under damp crumpled sheets. But nobody cared.

They drove to the beach every day and passed time pleasantly there. One morning, Flavio excused himself with a vague mumble and walked away. Joan didn't pay much attention. She lounged, read a book, went in and out of the water, and didn't became alarmed until she glanced and realized it was one o'clock. He must have disappeared around ten.

She packed up their beach bag and went into town to look for him in all the shops and cantinas. It took only a few minutes. The town was old and small; the church was a from Colonial times. Joan tried to describe Flavio to whomever she thought might understand either her English or her Spanish. They didn't think they had seen him, but would keep an eye out for him; no, no, it was no trouble at all. Some of them even did her the courtesy of calling her señora. The heat of the pavement burned her feet right through the thin rubber of her flip-flops. For a moment she felt as if somebody was watching her. It was the quizzical, concerned face of a truck driver who was fixing his vehicle by the side of the road. He looked as if he were about say something, but she didn't give him the chance. She ran off. She returned to the beach, but he wasn't there. She walked slowly with her bag slung over her bare, brown shoulder until she reached the road that lead to the nearby village where she and Flavio were staying.

She stood by the side of the road warily, trying to assess her chances of getting a ride from respectable people or tourists, but before she had a chance to make any kind of decision, an unshaven man in battered pick-up pulled up next to her and told her to hop in. She hesitated, but he reached over and opened the door so decisively that she felt it would be rude to refuse. They rode along in complete silence until they got to the town. "Aquí! Aquí!" she yelled.

He braked instantly, right in the middle of the road, and waited for her to get out. "Muchas gracias," she said, trying to sound as if she meant it.

In the main square of the village, across from the church, she found her own car unlocked and empty. Full of foreboding, but otherwise calm, she entered the courtyard of the hotel, if you could call it a hotel, and immediately noticed the sweet aroma of marijuana. The aroma led her right to her room.

Flavio sat in bed with Columbine, both in their underwear—Flavio in his old boxer shorts and the puppet in a white ruffled petticoat. "Why did you take her dress off?" asked Joan stupidly.

Flavio looked up at her with a slack jaw and red-rimmed eyes. Joan saw a paper bag full of marijuana on the floor. "I was dancing with her and…and…"

"And what?"

"She fall in the mud." He shrugged.

"You left me sitting on the beach like an idiot!" screamed Joan. It just burst out of her.

"But I was coming back!" He got up and tried to touch her. She brushed his hands off. "I was just getting ready to pick you up! Just now!"

"I was there for hours!" She began to sob.

"Yes, but I had work to do."

"What?"

"I was thinking of the puppet show! I have great ideas, magnificent ideas…I wrote them down…" He looked around in distracted desperation. "Ideas for us. I was thinking about us." She let him draw her into his arms and sobbed with anger against his sweaty skin. "Please, cara mia, now that we're together, I have to make a new show, no? A completely new show. So I have to make plans. Real plans. Anybody who knows me, knows my plans are serious."

"You like Columbine better than me," wept Joan.

"What? Columbine? Never!"

"Yes, you do!"

"Now you are silly. Don't be silly, my love. Don't do this. Don't."

His voice became an incantatory murmur. Indeed, she knew she was being silly, but it was such a tremendous relief to ignore the bleak obligations of rationality that had always stifled the fulfillment of her needs, to the point that she hardly remembered what she needed.

The next day she meekly asked him to give her some notion of this new show that he had planned, but he pouted at the request so she let it drop. It took them ten days to get back to Boston. They spent several days in Colorado, then crossed the monotonous surface of the Midwest in one long brutal stint of continual driving. One of them took the wheel while the other stretched out in the back seat. Joan felt strangely attached to this sleeping body. At least what she could see of it in the rearview mirror in the day or night. Nothing else in the world seemed real, only perhaps the voice of her sister, whom she already missed.

When they arrived at her apartment in Boston, they fell into bed for twelve hours and woke up at dawn. Flavio went off to find a dry cleaner for Columbine's dress. No use to explain that dry cleaners weren't open at 6:30 in the morning. He came back at noon with a dry cleaner's ticket and a pack of cigarettes. By the end of the day he had become a steady smoker. And she had embarked on her puppeteer training.

Joan had a mental list of things she wanted to do during the summer—art classes, furniture hunting, reading—but Flavio made short work of her plans. He gave her puppet-handling exercises, basic movements that she had to repeat over and over again, like playing scales on an instrument. When she had mastered some of these, he started teaching her routines—entire little choreo-graphed dances. When she asked if these dances were traditional or original, he shrugged, as if the distinction were either unclear or unimportant. He himself could make a marionette dance and talk with such agility and naturalness that he did not need to hide behind a curtain; the audience forgot him even when he was standing in plain sight. He had learned how to make puppets, and manipulate them, and throw his voice into them, in a school in Turin. But he could not stay in Italy, he said ruefully, because there were already too many talented people in his vocation."

"Profession," corrected Joan.

"I mean vocation, like, like a priest has a vocation."

While Joan tried to learn how to make Columbine waltz, Flavio set about to build a kind of miniature proscenium stage, a free-standing wooden frame that could be dismantled, transported, and reassembled. He shoved all the living room furniture into one corner in order to make room for his carpentry project; for a few weeks Joan's apartment was reduced to kitchen and a bedroom, separated by a big mess. Flavio even borrowed a sewing machine from one of her friends and made several beautiful curtains for his stage. The sewing took up less space, but he discouraged her from reclaiming the living room; he had plans to make a larger frame that would stand in front of the smaller one and hide the puppeteers behind a draped fringe.

Of course Joan had to pay for all the wood and all the fabric that he used. She didn't object, because he tried to do everything as cheaply as possible. She did object to the beer and wine he consumed, and refused to give him any more money for it. He didn't argue. He excused himself and returned hours later, smelling of alcohol. Did he have a secret fund somewhere or did he simply know how to cadge drinks in the local bar? She didn't ask. But she called up her sister and worried out loud about it. Martha said, in her balloon-popping tone of voice, "Please don't tell me that you're serious about that guy."

"Your comment is noted for the record," replied Joan. "I have been officially warned by you."

"Joanie, you don't know him."

"Yes I do—I'm getting to know him."

Martha snorted. "This guy…"

"He has a name."

"Fabuloso?"

"Flavio!"

"Whatever. You're only seeing the tip of the iceberg."

"How do you know?"

"It's the truth, that's how I know."

"I have to get going," said Joan, brusquely, ending the call.

One lazy morning, while perusing the newspaper, she read that a nearby college was going to sponsor an end-of-summer fair, a community event. When she told Flavio, he said, "Go there right now." So she went to the college and bumbled her way from office to office until she found somebody who claimed to be connected with the fair. She explained that she was a puppeteer and offered the services of her show. They told her to take a seat. Twenty minutes later, at the very moment she decided she had run out of patience, a smiling man asked her what her troupe was called. "Flavio's Gypsy Theater," she said immediately.

"Drop by the day before and we'll give you passes and find a place for you to set up. You'll be performing all day, right?"

"What about…money?"

"Sorry, we're already over budget. But hey, puppets don't eat! You don't have to feed 'em!" He went off chuckling.

"No money?" said Flavio when she returned. "Madonna! Arlecchino will go hungry! Never mind—you already agreed. Now we must practice."

They began rehearsing the show, or rather developing it, since he did not have every detail worked out, and in puppetry, the details make all the difference between delight and disenchantment. Since he did both voices, she had nothing to do but manipulate Columbine, but she literally had her hands full with this task. For the first time, he was displeased with her progress; she wasn't learning the moves fast enough. The idea of facing the public had transformed him from a genial teacher to a harsh, demanding colleague, or rather dictator, since he insisted on making all the decisions himself and rejecting all of Joan's suggestions, even the most reasonable. And since he was still revising the show, he would sometimes berate her for following directions that he had explicitly given her the day before. One night, feeling exhausted and harassed, Joan simply let the main control fall from her hand to the floor;

Columbine tumbled gracelessly onto her back.

"What are you doing!" cried Flavio. "The wires will tangle!"

"Fuck the wires," said Joan. She went into the bedroom, threw herself down on the bed, and cried. A moment later, the front door of the apartment slammed. He returned late the next afternoon, looking disheveled and sleepy. His eyelids were dark and almost swollen.

"Where did you spend the night, anyway?" said Joan. "Wait, I'll get you some coffee."

"In the park," he said.

When she brought him his coffee, she saw something more in his eyes than just a night in the park—an odd luster in his pupils.

"Are you stoned or something?" she said.

He shrugged and spread his hands out. "Sure, why not?" As soon as he finished his coffee he fell asleep with the cup in his hand, still sitting upright. Joan stretched him out so he would be comfortable. When he woke up, he said, "It is no good. We cannot work together."

"I love your puppets, but I need more time to practice. This pressure just takes all the fun out of it for me. Do we really have to put on this show that we're not even getting paid for?"

The question seemed to confuse him. He rubbed his eyes. "OK, OK, no need for problems. I find an assistant, maybe...I don t know where."

"Well, for chrissake, why don't you just advertise or look in the phone book or something. There must be somebody in this goddam city who knows how to make a puppet waltz!"

She put the phone book on the coffee table and opened it to Puppetry. There were only two listings. Flavio called them both and talked at length. When he was finished, he rushed into the shower and came out wearing his best clothes. Apparently, a local college had a kind of puppet division of their theater program, or so Joan deduced from Flavio's rather feverish description. He packed up the marionettes, borrowed her car keys, and went off in search of a new pair of hands.

A few hours later, he returned with the momentous news that he had found an assistant, a very talented college student who was willing to learn Columbine's part for the show. The next day, Joan helped Flavio dismantle the model stage and put it in the car. After that he was out every day rehearsing. So Joan got her living room and her solitude back all at once. It was a mixed feeling.

As the show approached, Joan decided to invite Flavio's assistant to have dinner with them. She was a nice girl, very energetic and very excited about Flavio's Italian style of handling puppets. The two of them began to talk about the commedia del'arte, the traditional street theater of mime, music and improvisation.

"Nobody knows what was the real commedia del'arte," said Flavio. "It finished in the eighteenth century. We have only what people wrote about it, and drawings."

The girl said, "No, it still lives in Italy"

"It does?" said Joan. "How?"

"How what?"

"How does the commedia del'arte still live in Italy?"

"Uh, I guess it's the…um, sense of style?"

Joan reached over and patted the girl on the head. The girl was like a bright child who can mimic adult sentences without really understanding them.

The day before the fair, Flavio showed up in the early afternoon. He was carrying the marionettes in his duffel bag. He was drunk and unreachable.

"What's wrong?" asked Joan.

"I am an artist, a director! I don't count votes!" His eyes were red. "What are you talking about?"

"I need a beer."

"That's the last thing you need!"

He left the room and came back with his beer and flopped on the couch in deep discontent. Try as she might, she couldn't get him to say anything. The thought crossed her mind that Flavio was just more trouble than he was worth.

The phone rang; Joan picked it up. It was Flavio's young assistant, sobbing wildly. Reluctantly, he took the phone and began to grunt answers to whatever questions she was putting to him. As he grunted, he turned his back to Joan and pulled the phone as far away from her as the curly cord would allow. Joan got the hint and went into her bedroom. She took up a novel and began to read. She kept reading the same paragraph over and over until she heard Flavio got off the phone.

"My dear, dear friend, I have good news and bad news."

"Don't talk to me in stupid clichés."

"Excuse me, my English is too simple. All I can use is the words I know."

"You know more than you let on."

He looked at her with sad brown eyes. "I am going away. I am going around United States with the puppet show. To many colleges and many schools."

"You are? When does this start?"

"In three days."

"You bastard! You're just leaving, just like that?"

"Not now. In three days."

"You sound like you're giving me notice. Do you think I'm your fucking employer?"

"Shh, not so loud," he said, pointing to the walls.

"Fuck the neighbors!"

Flavio shrugged. "They are your neighbors, not mine."

"You're going on tour with that college student, aren't you?" No answer. Joan said, "Take me instead."

Flavio said, "Impossible."

"I'll go anywhere you want."

Flavio said, "You have a home, a job. You must stay."

She began to cry. He sat down on the sofa and rubbed his eyes. Anything to avoid meeting her gaze. His discomfort made her uncomfortable, too. She made an effort to pull herself together.

"Christ, I need a drink," she said. "Do you want some vodka with cranberry juice?"

"Please."

"You sleep on the sofa tonight."

"Yes."

She went into the bedroom, slammed the door, and flopped on her bed.

She was exhausted and dozed off immediately. A crowd of people was laughing at her under a brilliant blue sky. The faces of children pressed close. She wanted to run away but couldn't move. Then a wire turned her head and she saw Arlecchino, looking beautiful in his silk outfit. And imposing, too; why, he was twice her size. "Don't you love me?" she heard herself say. He began to beat her with a wooden stick as the children shouted with excitement.

She woke in a sweat, the children's voices still buzzing in her head. The dream had been so vivid that waking up was like changing realities. But she felt refreshed. She now possessed a clarity that she realized had been missing for a long time. It was past six o'clock, still plenty of light. She walked into the living room. The phone cord stretched to the hall closet. She could hear Flavio's muffled voice. He was using the closet as a phone booth

She picked up Flavio's duffel bag and carried it outside. Her car was parked in the driveway—she only used the garage in winter. She took Arlecchino and laid him on the asphalt surface behind the rear left wheel of her car. She then put Colombine, with arms and legs spread out, behind the rear right wheel. Then she got in the car, put it in reverse, and drove over the marionettes. The sound of crunching was very satisfying, but when she had backed up enough to see the damage, she saw to her chagrin that the heads were still intact.

Flavio charged out the front door.

"Are you crazy?" he screamed. "Stop! Stop!"

She stopped. He approached the car. His look scared her. She said, "Touch me and you're going to jail! I'm warning you!"

"You touched my puppets! You broke them! You killed them!" He had tears in his eyes.

"You're a puppet maker. Make some new ones."

"I made them only with the help of a carpenter who lives in Torino. Here I cannot find even the right tools."

"I guess the tour is canceled, huh?" she said.

He began screaming. "I am leaving now! Now! Not tomorrow, not in three days, but right now!"

"If you take anything that's not yours, I'm calling the police."

He shouted something in Italian and stomped into the house. It took him less than an hour to collect the bits and pieces of his transient existence and pack them into his backpack. He looked genuinely miserable.

"Are you going over to your assistant's place?" The question just popped out of Joan's mouth.

"Yes. She understands me. She is not cruel. She is not somebody who destroys precious things. She is not full of revenge and hate."

"I'll give you a ride," said Joan That was the fastest way to get rid of him. They went to the car. Flavio opened the back door, threw his backpack in, and went around to the front seat. He was angry. They rode in silence. When Joan stopped the car in front of the college dormitory, Flavio dropped his set of her house keys into her lap.

"Thanks, I forgot you had them," she said. He grabbed his backpack and a plastic shopping bag that she hadn't noticed before.

"Wait. What's in that bag?"

He spoke with the solemnity of a priest at a funeral. "These are the heads of Arlecchino and Colombine."

To his horror, she burst out laughing, shattering the complacency of the drowsy street.

The Returns

I needed a job, but there were none. It was the late seventies, and papers were raging about the Iran hostage crisis, gas shortages, and recession. It felt like a giant hangover after a failed revolution, the harsh morning after ebullient years of rebellion, experimentation, and self-indulgence. The party was over.

But I wasn't prepared to deal with reality yet. I entered grad school at Syracuse University. My teaching stipend kept me alive...but only while I was actually teaching. I didn't get paid during the summer. And I had no financial help from anyone. My father was well-off, but wasn't about to help support me and my frivolous pursuits, which he had deeply disapproved of ever since I learned to walk and talk.

I studied the shrinking want-ads section of the newspaper. I called people. I wore out my good shoes going to offices and leaving my resume with secretaries whose blank eyes told me not to hope. When I dropped into McDonald's to inquire about a position, there were more people waiting on line for application forms than for cheeseburgers.

It was a golden spring. The very loveliness of May seemed to mock my bad luck. Now that most of the students were gone, a stillness pervaded the streets in the university area, including Fraternity Row, with its great leafy elms and well-tended lawns. Birds practically rioted in the eaves every morning. I met a pale, dark-haired Jewish woman named Lori over wine and cheese following a tedious lecture. She invited me to come by and watch TV with her and I couldn't think of a single reason not to. I dropped by her place a few days later, with a small cake I really couldn't afford. Lori talked a lot but I didn't listen to most of it. I was watching TV—I didn't own one. The evening was a great success for both of us.

I started dropping by two or three times a week. She couldn't seem to resist the neurotic compulsion to ventilate her problems in great detail, but was nervous about revealing so much about herself. I provided just the right amount of benevolent inattention. But one rainy night I must have been skimping on the benevolence or overdoing the inattention, because Lori sharply reproached me for being moody and self-absorbed.

We were watching a documentary about octopuses—thrashing tentacles and frothy bubbles.

I told her I was worried about finding a job.

She frowned for a moment and twirled a strand of her long dark hair around her fingers. A friend of hers worked as a reporter for the evening newspaper, the Syracuse Herald-Journal. She would give him a call in the morning and tell him to hire me. "Is that what you want?" she said.

"Yeah!" I said.

"OK, then," she said.

And having solved all my problems, she went right back to complaining about her own life: her father's ambition to see her go to grad school and her mother's desire to see her get married and her own confusion about what to do. She worked in the office of the Dean of Students and liked it because it demanded so little from her. Grad school would be a lot of pressure, wouldn't it? I could only think about the newspaper job. Did they need a copy editor? A junior reporter? I had a degree in English under my belt. Meanwhile, on TV, a scuba diver in a cage was being lowered into the multiple embrace of a giant squid, but I failed to get the message.

As soon it was late enough to make a polite exit, I yawned ostentatiously and thanked Lori for a nice evening. She insisted on accompanying me to the door. The tall hedges that flanked her front door glistened with raindrops and exuded the freshness of new foliage. As soon as I took the first turn in the hedges, I heard Lori say, "Yoo hoo! Yoo hoo!" First I thought her cat had gotten loose, so I went back through the hedges to see if I could round up the animal. Instead, I ran into Lori, who pasted herself against my body and smooched me with more enthusiasm than passion. It was quite a surprise, but just as I started to get used to the idea, she broke the clinch, still panting, her glasses askew, and slammed the door in my face.

In the morning I called her at work and reminded her to speak to her friend at the newspaper. Of course she had completely forgotten about it, and sounded cross. But she called me back later and told me to show up the following afternoon at the cafeteria of the Herald-Journal. Her friend Lucian would be waiting for me there.

That evening, I went to see Lori again. This time the goodbye kiss was not a surprise attack, but a gentle overture, a lingering promise. When I emerged from the hedges around her front door, the stars and the porch lights and the fireflies in the grass glimmered enchantingly. I was about to acquire both a girlfriend and a job at the same time. For me, it was a conjunction as rare as a total eclipse of the sun.

The following day I quickly threw together a new resume that emphasized my writing skills, put on my only good suit coat, and showed up at the cafeteria of the newspaper at 3 p.m. as scheduled. The day was unusually hot for early June and I was sweating by the time I arrived. I asked around for Lucian and found him having a cup of coffee and a sandwich. He was about my age, rather stiff and serious, but amiable. "Excuse me for eating in front of you," he said.

"This is my breakfast. I work the evening shift."

"So Lori tells me you're a reporter."

"That's right. I live in Liverpool." That meant he was a rising young professional.

"I'm a teaching assistant in the English department," I said, "but I need something to tide me over the summer. I thought with all my experience writing…"

Something in his expression deflated the rest of my pitch. He led me to another table and introduced me to a squinting rotund woman whose hair was pulled up into a bun. A cigarette clung to her bottom lip. She looked at me with point-blank suspicion.

"This is Dottie. She can explain everything to you. I better get back to my desk. Say hello to Lori for me."

"Sure will!" I said. "Thanks a million!" My armpits dripped sweat. I asked Dottie if she'd like to see my resume.

"Got any sales experience?" she asked.

"Oh, here and there," I said. "The usual."

"How do you feel about selling newspaper subscriptions door to door? Think you can handle it? Salary plus commission. You got a car?"

I shook my head apologetically. She gave an equine snort and said, "We'll find transportation for you. Come back here at 5 p.m."

At 5 p.m. I was in the cafeteria again, sitting at a table with about ten guys and a couple of women. They were all small-town residents. Dottie appointed four drivers and assigned the rest of us to their cars. The drivers got gasoline allowances, but they still complained that their assignments were too far away. "Be glad I ain't sending you to Rochester," growled Dottie. We were given brand-new clipboards with sheets of coupons and subscription forms.

Soon I found myself sitting in the back of an old white Camaro with a twenty-one-year-old kid named Roger.

"So what do we have to do, Roger?"

"Go from door to door and get people to sign up for subscriptions. If they sign up, they get four, fifty-percent-off coupons. If they already have a subscription, don't give them any coupons. You have to sell at least five subscriptions a night. If somebody changes their mind and doesn't want to pay for his subscription, that's called a Return. They expect you to have some Returns, but if you get too many, you're out of here."

The driver dropped Roger and me on a street corner and said he'd be back at eight-thirty. He drove off blasting Johnny Cash from his eight-track car stereo.

"Gotta move it!" said Roger through gritted teeth, and he charged down the street like a solidier into battle. I trudged toward the nearest of a row of identical apartment buildings. Everything was new. Even the lawns had been planted in newly imported dirt. I began ringing doorbells. In every apartment I saw boxes along the wall, cabinets that still had manufacturer's labels stuck on them, brand-new televisions. Had they all moved in the day before? People would answer the door with vaguely disoriented expressions, as if caught in free fall. Some of them asked me little questions to determine if I were an intruder from the outside world or just another annoying feature of the place. It felt awkward to be interrupting people at dinner but also by the oppressive impermanence of the place. But I had done well on my first night out.

"I sold seven subscriptions," I said to Roger proudly.

"I sold thirteen," he said.

"How did you do that?" He shrugged.

The following evening, Tuesday, I sold five and he sold twelve. On Wednesday evening I sold seven and he sold seventeen. On Thursday I sold only four, even though I begged and pleaded with the customers and made self-deprecating jokes and promised extra coupons. Roger sold nineteen subscriptions that night, working just across the street from me. I always seemed to be on the wrong side of the block.

Our driver was even less of a salesman than I was. He was about forty years old, and we found him already there, smoking a cigarette and listening to Tammy Wynette with a faraway look in his eyes. He quit at the end of the week.

Come Friday, I got my first paycheck. It was small, but it was enough to invite Lori to see the weekend film at the campus auditorium. They were showing Woody Allen's "Love and Death"—one of his best. Everybody was rolling in the aisles, but Lori didn't crack a smile. She told me several times, in a vehement whisper, that Woody Allen was ugly. At first I wondered if this was an indirect way of telling me I was handsome. But it didn't feel like a compliment.

Fortunately, when the lights went back on, Lori forgot about Woody Allen. She became high-spirited, almost giddy, and together we skipped back to her apartment hand in hand, or rather, she skipped and I bounded along just to humor her. We went to her bedroom and she lay back like the Queen of Sheba, ready for the royal treatment. I tried to oblige her. I hefted her to one side and unbuttoned her, then I rolled her to the other side and unzipped her. She said, "You forgot something," and tapped on her glasses with her finger, so I removed them gently and put them on the night table.

By now I was so steamed up that I could have raped a pit bull, but I still had to get her panties off, and she wasn't helping at all, only giggling a little.

I pulled at the panties but they got all balled up around her thighs. I wondered why she didn't arch her back or do something to contribute to what I had always regarded as a collaborative effort. With one mighty jerk I tugged the panties off, raising her backside and then dropping it again like a sack of potatoes. The recoil almost threw me off the bed.

"Ouchie," she said, frowning.

I climbed aboard her and stroked her hair. "Where does it hurt?" I said in a gooey, baby-talk voice. She gave me a dead serious look.

"I better tell you right now—I have a hard time coming."

Well, that was my invitation to make her rock and roll, but though I tried everything, I only succeeded in driving myself wild. Lori remained unresponsive, almost aloof.

In the morning I sat in her sunny kitchen consuming scrambled eggs, toast and orange juice faster than she could put it on the table. I couldn't help noticing airs of disappointment escaping from her now and then, but Lori's little sighs bothered me no more than faraway clouds in a big blue sky. Then the clouds got bigger and darker and the wind began to blow. It turned out she had taken some work home and was dreading it. She asked me to stay with her, but I made up some excuse and went home and spent the rest of the day smoking pot and playing guitar.

That week Dottie assigned me to another car. My new driver was not much older than me. He said, "It don't matter what you're selling, cause in the end, you are both the seller and the product." That was the whole he secret of success. Be your own pimp.

The driver sat hunched over the wheel, baseball cap tilted forward, his whole demeanor radiating tension. He must have sensed that I thought he was an imbecile, because he turned to me and said, "You don't believe me, do ya? What would you say if I told you that you was going to have the greatest sales evening of your life tonight?"

I said, "Yeah, right."

He shook his head. "I guess I'm just gonna have to prove it to you." He could barely conceal his excitement. I looked around to see what there was to get excited about. It was 5:15 p.m. on a Monday night. We were headed south down Salina Street, but instead of continuing in that direction, he pulled sharply into the heart of the South Side ghetto.

"What are we doing here?" I asked.

"Selling newspapers," the driver said, pulling over.

I was about to object, but what difference did it make if I annoyed the people in this neighborhood or some other?

"Meet you all back here at eight," he said.

Armed with our clipboards and coupons, we fanned out along the street. The very first door I knocked on yielded a sale. A black family stopped eating dinner when I showed up and exchanged a quick, whispered conversation. The family spoke to me courteously and ended up buying a subscription.

I couldn't help thinking about the kind of reception a young black man would get if he went round ringing doorbells in a white neighborhood.

Two doors down, I sold another subscription. And then another.

In the lobby of a dilapidated apartment building I met a bone-thin, white-haired man who wore both suspenders and belt because he had no ass to hang his trousers on. He filled out the subscription form, and insisted on taking me to a friend's place so that he could get a subscription, too.

"Bin years since you could get a paper delivered round here," said the old man. "You gots to go to the drugstore for it and half the time they ain't got it." He spat on the ground.

His crony bought a subscription and they turned me back loose into the street. From then on, my sales job turned into a party. People were filling out subscription forms with a smile, shaking my hand, and generally carrying on as if I was giving out free ice cream. I sold twenty-two that night. When I got back to the car, the driver was grinning with such intensity that I wondered if he were a little mad or perhaps on a manic high. But he only wanted me to admit that he was right and I was wrong, and, under the circumstances, I was perfectly willing to oblige him.

When we got back to the Herald-Journal building, we waltzed into the cafeteria and made a big deal out of presenting our subscription forms to Dottie, who sat immobile at her usual table like some kind of Buddha with a cold-creamed face and dangling cigarette. She gathered our forms, glanced at one after another, then tossed them all in the plastic garbage can. We were stunned.

"We don't deliver to that part of town," she said.

"Why not?" I said. "They wanted newspapers. They were ready to pay for them."

"Go argue with the circulation department if you don't like it. Meanwhile, I'll overlook the fact you didn't go where I sent you, but you better not try it again."

One of my fellow passengers said, "It wasn't my idea, it was the driver. He took me there."

We turned around to look at the driver and realized that he was gone—gone forever, as it turned out.

"I don't care whose idea it was," said Dottie. "Just so long as you go where I send you next time."

The rest of the week, I had to scramble to make up for that evening.

On Friday night, I offered to take Lori to the movies again. Fortunately, that weekend's campus movie wasn't a comedy—it was the old classic "A Streetcar Named Desire." I was so absorbed that I didn't notice Lori's reaction until the lights went up.

"Did you like it?" I asked.

"That was horrible!"

"What!" I said. "You didn't at least think the acting was good?"

"The way he treated her! It was so awful!"

As we walked home, she kept about a yard away from me. If I tried to move closer to her, she would swerve away. Sometimes she would swerve for no particular reason.

"I still can't believe what he did to her."

I felt sure that the night was over, but when we got to her place, she said, "Well, let's go to bed."

We went into her bedroom, pulled each other's clothes off and went at it.

But she remained tense and rigid. She said, "There's something..."

"What? What is it?"

"I'm a little embarrassed…"

"For what? Just say it, whatever you want."

"I don't know if I can just say it."

What dark desire was she holding back? Belts, whips, who knows, maybe that big carrot in the bottom of the fridge?

"Please, honey, don't be afraid to tell me what you want," I whispered.

"OK," she said, and shoved my head into her crotch.

Nothing I tried could make her abandon herself and wallow in the unconsciousness of coming.

In the morning Lori was grateful, embarrassed, and disappointed. She insisted I spend the day with her, and I acquiesced, but I refused to go shopping with her in the afternoon. Instead, I sat in her living room and read. During those two hours, while she was shopping and I was reading, our relationship was at its best. When she returned, however, things took a turn for the worse.

She complained about shopping alone and having to carry the bags all the way home by herself. I tried to help her put the food away, but kept putting things in the wrong place, and she came close to having a tantrum. When she started looking through the TV Guide, it was my turn to have a tantrum.

"It's not even seven o'clock and you're already planning to start watching TV? Give me a break!"

"Well, this is a surprise. What do you want to do?"

"Anything. Get high, take a walk around the park."

She sat down and stretched out on the couch. "I don't feel like wandering around at night."

She picked up the clicker and turned on the TV. I went home and plucked at my Gibson guitar for a while with only half a heart. My blues didn't sound bluesy; they came out depressed and funereal.

To make matters worse, that week's sales were terrible. I sold only nine subscriptions in three days. Out of desperation I filled out several bogus subscription forms, figuring that later sales would compensate for a few Returns.

On Thursday afternoon, Dottie sent us to Auburn, New York, a small town outside Syracuse. She said we would each be assigned to a local partner, someone who actually lived in the town, but all the subscriptions we sold would count toward our salary and commission as usual. Apparently, the newspaper really wanted to break into this market.

Auburn is built around a large penitentiary that happens to be the town's largest employer. It is difficult to imagine a more totalitarian example of civic planning. The center of town is dominated by high gray walls. Half the vehicles here are police cars from various law enforcement agencies and the other half are paddy wagons transporting convicts to and from other places. We drove around the prison—there's nowhere else to go in Auburn.

At that moment, a small memory just popped into my head. I remembered that I had a joint in my pocket. Which was a felony in those days.

The driver dropped me off at an old frame house where my local contact sat on the front porch steps waiting for me, waving cheerfully and showing off her legs. She was a tall, blonde, and high-breasted girl of fourteen or fifteen. As we walked from house to house, she chattered away. "That's where the Rayburns live—they have five kids. Bonnie Rayburn's in my class. Have you ever been to the Onondaga County fair? Bonnie promised to take me to the fair in August. Don't tell my Dad, he'd kill me if he knew. He says people just get drunk and fight there. There must be an awful lot of boys. there." She giggled. "Bonnie's supposed to get her permit in July. There's Skip Wright! Hey, Skip, is your mom at home?"

A boy on a bicycle shook his head as he pedaled along, or maybe he just shook the hair out of his eyes. The street was, I had to admit, pleasant enough.

Old, arching maple trees, white houses with large front porches, so little traffic that we could walk in the middle of the road.

"Do you have a car?" she said.

"No!" I said.

"Why not?"

"I just don't need one."

"You must be crazy, mister."

"That's what my doctor keep telling me."

She inhaled sharply. Then she broke into a smile. "You're just pulling my leg, ain't ya?"

"You caught me. You're an alert young lady."

We stopped at a lot of houses and everybody was very friendly and neighborly with my local contact and very cool with me. Sometimes she didn't even mention the word "subscription." When I asked her why, she said, "They're too busy to read the newspaper, it's not even worth trying." She did sell one or two subscriptions, but not in front of me. I waited on the porch while she went inside to have a glass of pink lemonade and clinch the deal. As we walked from street to street, she kept brushing against my arm with her boobs. After a while I was practically dancing around her to avoid touching her. She became bored and said, "Well, I got to practice my piano now, cause my mom says any girl who wants to win a beauty contest has be more than just good-looking, she's got to be talented some way or other. I thought, well, music is a talent and everyone likes music. So let's go back to my house and you can wait for your friends to come and get you."

I would have preferred to keep selling subscriptions, but I didn't argue. When we got back to her house she stopped at the front lawn. When I asked to use the bathroom, she said, "It's inside. My father will show you." With some trepidation I opened the screen door and walked into one of the messiest dining rooms I've ever seen. The table and sideboard were crowded with empty Coke bottles and milk cartons; brown paper bags almost covered the hook rug on the floor; heaps of butts buried the ashtrays. On the other side of the table, in a rocking chair, sat a thin, grim-faced man with a bushy gray moustache. He wore a frayed t-shirt, dungarees with suspenders, and a State Highway Patrol hat with a badge pinned to it. He peered at me over his spectacles.

"Who are you?" he said, without the slightest hint of welcome in his voice.

I nervously explained that I sold subscriptions for the Syracuse newspaper, and that his daughter had told me I could come in to use the bathroom.

Keeping one eye on me, he walked to the window, bent open the aluminum slats of the Venetian blind, and peered outside. The girl was gone. I realized that the man had an enormous revolver stuck in the back of his belt, a gun that could topple a bear. He slowly turned and indicated the hallway with a tilt of the head. "John's down there, last door on the left."

When I came out of the bathroom, he was back in his rocking chair, doing nothing. Nothing at all.

I sat down on the porch and filled out some subscription forms for such avid newspaper readers as Emma Bovary, Leopold Bloom, and Blanche Dubois.

That weekend I didn't call Lori and she didn't call me. All my psychic energy went into the black hole of not speaking to Lori, not phoning her. It was exhausting.

She called in the middle of the week.

"Come over," she said, sounding upset. "I don't want to be alone tonight."

We began to kiss as soon as I walked in her front door. We barely stopped to say hello. She guided me by the hand into her bedroom and we shed our clothes quickly and eagerly. As soon as I got in bed with her, she said, "I want to have an orgasm."

After about 45 minutes of trying and agonizing but not getting there, I finally rolled over and said, "Lori, honey, I can't do this any more."

"Well, that's just great!" she barked. There were tears in her eyes. Her alarm woke us up early. It was a working day.

At first we didn't know what to say to each other. Neither one of us wanted to allude to the night before. As I pulled on my jeans, I said, "Are you free this weekend?" Which implied that I wanted to see her—but that was a lie.

"No, I'm busy this weekend," she lied.

"Too bad," I lied.

"Maybe some other weekend," she lied.

"Any time," I lied.

"I'll give you a call when I have some free time," she lied.

We had both utterly lost interest in the relationship; nothing was left, not even resentment. All we shared was a desire to separate with minimum fuss. Already Lori's attention was turned on what to wear for work. While she was going through her closet, I just walked out of her house. It was another beautiful early summer's day. My jaw ached.

A few hours later, when I arrived at the newspaper's cafeteria, I ran into Lucian.

"Hello, there," he said. "How's Lori?"

What could I say? "Fine."

He yawned. "Boy, am I tired. I was up all night writing up an interview I did with the Mayor. I've got to meet with all the top county Republicans next week. And how's your job going?"

"I've meeting both Republicans and Democrats. Some independents, too."

"I'm going to eat my sandwich now," he said, and dismissed me with a little wave of the hand.

Dottie dispatched the car that I was riding to the furthest edge of the subscription map, an area that looked suburban but was really a peripheral suburbia sprawled out in rural countryside. There was even a scent of manure in the air. When the car let me off by the side of the highway. I quickly realized that selling my quota of subscriptions would not be easy. Not only were the houses separated by enormous lawns, but each one sat at the end of a long asphalt driveway, well away from the road. It took five to ten minutes of walking to get from one door to the next.

Nobody answered the door at the first house, nor at the second.

I began looking at the houses more carefully. They were large. Someone could be doing the laundry or the dishes somewhere inside and not hear the doorbell. They might not even expect to hear it. People around here probably didn't drop in on their neighbors. It would be easier to get in a car and drive to the nearest grocery store than to hike over five acres of lawn to borrow a cup of sugar.

Anyway, I started ringing doorbells for longer and longer periods of time. At first I was nervous about annoying somebody, but after a few more closed doors, I just wanted to see another face, even an unpleasant one. I jabbed at the same doorbell again and again. Was I alone out here? Next house, I kept my finger pressed to the bell and heard it jangling within for many long minutes. Had everybody been kidnapped by aliens or evacuated in an emergency? And yet no place looked less like an emergency. I passed cars and tricycles, basketball hoops over garage doors and heavy curtains evidently meant to discourage nosy blue jays, because nobody in the neighborhood could peer into anybody else's window without high-powered binoculars. The houses were too far apart.

As I was walking down a looping road that appeared to be leading me back to the main highway, I finally ran into another living creature—a big, mean dog. The dog bared his teeth when he saw me and began to bark aggressively. I retreated slowly and carefully but the dog followed, snapping and snarling. I tried to suppress an urge to run or make any sudden movements. The dog continued to bark at me and came within attack distance. My only weapon was my clipboard. Fear pumped violently through my body and my heart beat hard. Out of the corner of my eye I saw a man with a plaid shirt strolling down the road. I wanted to tell him to get a stick or do something, but was afraid that shouting would further aggravate the dog. For what seemed an eternity of terror, the beast barked and snarled at me, his whole frame poised to leap forward.

The man in the plaid shirt whistled and the dog trotted off.

I realized I was shaking and drenched in sweat. Not exactly the best way to make a favorable impression on potential customers. I turned around and walked down one road, then another, until I reached a grassy ridge. I made my way to the top and sat down in the long shadows of the setting sun, where I could see the houses clustered below me, and beyond that an interstate highway that promised other destinations, some of them better. I found half a joint in my pocket and smoked it. Then I clicked my ballpoint pen a few times, filled out a few subscription forms, and then began to write a poem about the twilight. Any day now, the newspaper's circulation department would find out that Gustave Flaubert, Ezra Pound, and Virginia Woolf had signed up but did not intend to pay for eight weeks of the Syracuse Herald-Journal. Dostoevsky wouldn't subscribe even at the low introductory rate. One of these days, Dottie would summon me to her table and tell me, to my vast and secret relief, that my Returns had come in. And then I will experience the bliss of being rid of both job and girlfriend.

Lady Taliban lip-syncs at the Kabul Cabaret

Secret Diaries of Jacques Casanova

Though I sit at his table, I am no better than a dancing bear. Unfortunately, having run out of money and prospects, not to mention youth, I must accept my lot. The kitchen lackeys torment me; they deliberately serve my macaroni cold and bring me inferior wine. The dogs bark directly beneath my window at night. The priest tries to convert me with inane arguments, as if I should be stupider in my old age. The Count himself sometimes neglects to introduce me to distinguished visitors, and when he does so, he says, "This is the famous, or should I say notorious, Jacques Casanova," with a laugh that precludes respect.

Let them say what they will. I have more important things to do. I have embarked on the project of assembling a history of my life, and to this end I sit in the library and write for thirteen hours a day, rain or shine. In the process of recalling the details of my experience, I have been transformed from participant to observer, from actor to audience. I might even add from defendant to judge, for he who lives in the thick of action must defend himself, whereas judgment is the privilege of the detached.

Venice, July 1758
Hearing news that the Contessa Sofia della R— had returned to the city, I made haste to pay her a visit and rekindle our former friendship, but the lackey who opened the door to me told me firmly that the Contessa could not receive me. However, he said if I showed up at the gardens of the Duke the following night, and sought her as Apollo sought for Cupid, I might be favored with an encounter.

Of course all of Venetian society knew that the Duke was throwing a masked ball on his ancestral estate. When I arrived, it was late; there was already a line of elegant coaches; indeed, some of the coachman were so splendidly attired that they could have passed for nobility themselves. I was dressed as Apollo, as suggested, and wore a white satin mask over my face. The party was a swirl of costumes, torchlight, and music, but I paid little attention, being obsessed with the desire to see my Sofia again. I pushed back and forth through the crowd until I beheld a lovely masked Cupid adorned with little wings, a bow, and a quiver of arrows, gliding along the floor as if she were above, rather than inside, the throng. Straightaway I approached her and suggested a quiet stroll along garden paths, away from the crush of boisterous revelers. She eagerly assented. I took her hand, warm and pliant, into mine. When we arrived at a secluded spot, I said, "Now you can remove your mask, my darling!"

She pulled her silver mask off her face. To my surprise, it wasn't her!

Then I removed my own mask—and to her surprise, it wasn't me! Neither she nor I knew who we were.

Avignon, April 1761

At dinner I found myself sitting next to the young wife of the Chevalier de M——. Her name was Jeanne. She was a charming dark-eyed young woman with a certain air of sadness. I teased her about this, asking whether she regretted the food or the company. She replied that, au contraire, it was the thought that she must depart soon that made her gloomy. She had very few opportunities to amuse herself. Her husband left her alone at home for days on end, but forbade her from going out. She had no company but some female servants and one very childish grandmother, so she was often bored to desperation. It was worse than a convent, she said.

—I will be glad to visit you anytime you like, and I promise not to bore you, I said.

At this she turned pale, saying that it was impossible for any man to visit her, because the neighbors or the servants would certainly tell her husband, and he was not one to let an injury pass unavenged.

—Don't tell me people around here really spy on each other's visitors!

—M. Casanova, this is not Paris, she replied.

—I will keep that in mind. I ask you only to think of me at 3 o'clock tomorrow afternoon.

I bowed, and she gave me a look that combined interest and trepidation.

The next morning, I went to a tailor and had him make me an entire set of female garments. After he fitted me, I shaved carefully, doused myself with perfume, and powdered my face, greatly assisted by the tailor's daughter. I emerged from the tailor dressed as a woman of fashion and hailed a carriage. At about 3 p.m. I arrived at the large and imposing house of the Chevalier de M——. The door opened immediately and Jeanne pulled me inside. She had been waiting for me.

—Come upstairs before the servants return. I sent them all out on errands.

As soon as we entered her boudoir, she shut the door and began laughing. I caught sight of myself in the mirror and began laughing also. But she put her finger to my lips to silence me.

—You are too foolish, too reckless! My husband could have you excommunicated, jailed, sent to the galleys, anything he wants.

I took her in my arms and kissed her. She removed my powdered and be-ribboned wig and dropped it on the floor. Then we began to undress each other.

As Jeanne removed my taffeta coat, my overdress, and my petticoats, I began to feel more like a woman than a man, but no less excited for all that.

Afterwards, we helped each other dress again. We adjusted each other's folds, just as playful as two little maidens in a garden. Jeanne reapplied my makeup, humming pleasantly as she hovered over me.

That moment, her husband, the Chevalier, strode into the boudoir, wearing his high boots and tapping his palm with a riding crop, for he was returning from a hunting party.

—What's going on here?

He barked out his words like an irritable dog. But Jeanne replied with a cheerful insouciance.

—Dear, I am teaching M. Casanova how to apply makeup.

—What the devil for?

—Because he wants to learn, that's why.

—That's enough. Get out of here.

—Why? This is my room!

—I said leave! I wish to speak to your friend!

Jeanne fluttered out of the room. As soon as she closed the door behind her, the Chevalier threw himself on me and covered my face with kisses. And I had to submit to his passion, even welcome it, so as not to raise the Chevalier's suspicions about my presence in his wife's intimate chamber. So I was undressed a second time that afternoon.

And twice the next day, too.

Parma, September 1763

As I was sitting in the dining room of an inn one afternoon, a magnificent carriage pulled up to the door and a fine lady, accompanied by some family members, entered the inn. Indeed, the whole party was so well dressed and well bred that I could not help wondering what had brought them to such an inn, which was respectable but hardly fashionable.

As the wife of the innkeeper bustled around her distinguished guests, I expressed my curiosity to a diner at the next table.

—Oh, that's the Donna S—. She lives close by. Her house is full of ghosts. She often comes here just to get away from them.

Upon hearing those words, I jumped up and introduced myself to the Donna, for I am not slow when I sense the opportunity to win the favor of a rich and aristocratic lady.

—I hope I am not disturbing you (I said with a bow), but I wish to pay my respects to you and your companions. My name is Giacomo Casanova, adept in the occult arts, Cabala scholar, exorcist, alchemist, astrologer, freemason, and Rosicrucian.

—Exorcist? said the Donna. Her voice dropped low.

—We have a problem, Signor Casanova, that you may be able to help us with. I assure you that success will be richly rewarded.

—The honor of serving you will be my reward.

—We shall see.

Turning to the rest of the table, the Donna said,

—I am stepping out for a moment. Do not disturb yourselves.

Donna S— told me to enter her carriage and ordered the driver to take us back to her castle. During the ride she explained to me that two cousins of hers, a brother and sister, had been killed in the castle not more than a year ago, but their spirits would not quit the premises, despite a liberal application of priests, crucifixes, and holy water. When I inquired as to who perpetrated this horrendous double murder, and for what reason, the Donna blushed and would not look at me. Clearly, the topic was a delicate one, so I let it go and asked how exactly the spirits made their presence known to the living. Donna S— told me that they sometimes made an unholy racket and frightened everybody.

—What kind of racket? I asked.

—They tip over chairs, break good dishes, curse the saints…it makes my blood run cold…I can't stand it anymore! All our servants have run away!

I instructed the Donna to leave me alone in the castle. I needn't have bothered—she had no intention of setting foot past the threshold. The castle was enormous, silent. I roamed the corridors admiring the furniture and the fine paintings. At last I came to the room where the assassinations had obviously taken place. A black curtain hung in front of the door. The door was unlocked, but the room had apparently not been entered, or even dusted, for a long time. I had to open the windows to relieve the stuffiness. Faint traceries of cobweb hung from the corners of the ceiling. I blew the dust off the desk, found ink and paper, and began to scribble occult formulas that I remembered from the Cabala and Paracelsus. As the evening light waned, I lit a candle. I began to tire, and almost dropped off to sleep, but some sound startled me awake. A soft moan, perhaps, but so quiet, it might have been a trick of the wind. The candle's flame remained steady.

Then I heard a louder moan. I jumped up, pulled a crucifix off the wall, and brandished it like a sword in front of me.

A hand caressed the back of my neck.

—Jesus save me! I cried, and leaped halfway across the room. The candlestick flew off the desk and clattered to the floor.

—Who are you? I cried. What do you want?

—If you will listen, we will speak, said a woman's voice, emanating from I knew not where. I shook with fear, gripping the crucifix with all my strength, as if it were some branch that might keep me from falling.

—Speak, then, I said, trying to sound steady and unaffected.

—What is your name? said a deep male voice.

—Giacomo Casanova.

—Casanova, are you a good man?

—That question is not for me to answer.

—Casanova, do you have a generous nature?

—My heart and my purse are often open.

—Listen to our story then, said the baritone voice in the darkness. I am named Gianotto, and my sister is named Magdalena. We were born two years apart and I am the eldest. The birth of my sister was the death of our mother, as happens so often in this sad world. Our father, feeling that he was not able to take care of two infants, planned to send us away to live with his relatives in a mountain village. He put my sister in the wagon first, but at the last moment he changed his mind and held on to me. So my sister was sent away while I stayed here. I always knew I had a sister, but we had been separated so young that I had no memory of her at all, just my father holding me in his arms as the wagon rolled away. The years went by.

One cursed day, when I was grown man, I returned from hunting in the afternoon and found a number of guests in the castle. This was nothing unusual, nor was it strange to find out that the visitors were distant relatives. What made this visit extraordinary was one of the visitors, a shy but beautiful young woman. I fell in love with her the moment I saw her, and she with me. For three days, we experienced pure bliss, which we kept secret from the rest of the family, for we wanted to be alone together.

Then, at dinner on the third night, my father pointed to me and to my beloved, and announced that we were brother and sister, now reunited after many years, and indeed, the whole purpose of the visit was to surprise the two of us with the renewal of our long-lost family bond. I felt the blood rush out of my head, leaving me deathly pale, no doubt.

My sister fainted, which caused a great commotion. Father reproached himself for breaking the news in such an abrupt and public manner, but he imagined that it would only bring us both joy, not an inferno of pain and remorse. To make the tale short, we played our family roles quite properly in the light of day, but we could not stay away from each other at night. We trespassed, and we repented, and we sinned again. One night we were discovered in bed by a hot-headed young cousin. He did not give us a chance to confess or receive last rites. He drew his sword and dispatched us as we were, in a state of sin. Now our unshriven souls are trapped on earth.

—You are not in hell?

—Hell is the loss of joy. Do you understand?

—I think so.

—And our sin, do you understand that as well?

—I have seen enough of the world to say yes, I understand.

—Could you forgive such a sin? So our holy church calls it: a mortal sin.

—But I am a freethinker, and I freely forgive you for your actions, which seem to be the result of bad luck more than anything else.

—Casanova, said the woman's voice. You have freed us from earth. All we needed was one living person to forgive us. I must have lost consciousness at that moment. When I woke up, it was dawn already, and I was lying on the floor. I staggered to my feet and rushed out of the house, running until I finally threw myself in tall grass and breathed the bright morning sky into my lungs.

Madrid, May 1766

Nowhere in Europe is the church so strict and the women such libertines as in Spain.

One Sunday in the cathedral, I asked my friend Don Pedro about a slender dark-haired beauty who sat a few rows ahead of us. He laughed at my question.

—That is Señorita Ignacia. Her family is very powerful and they're looking for a suitable match for her. In the meanwhile, I advise you to chase any other petticoats but hers.

—But I'm interested in her.

—That may be, but why should she be interested in you?

—Alright, let's make a little bet, I said. I'll wager you that I can have her in two weeks. My proof will be that I have one of her rings in my possession.

—Done! It will cost you money to learn to the lesson of humility, my friend, and I will be happy to collect the fee.

We shook hands and I left Don Pedro so I could follow Señorita Ignacia and discover where she lived. She was accompanied by her duenna wherever she went, and the presence of this professional chaperon made my enterprise more dangerous—but more exciting.

The next day I purchased the most exquisite fan I could find. I stood in the street where Señorita Ignacia lived, and when she came out of her house, I ran after her.

—Señorita, I shouted. You lost something. She stopped and made a gesture to her duenna.

—What have I lost? she asked.

I spread the fan, bowed, and introduced myself by name as a gentleman from Italy.

—This is not my fan, Señor, though I wish it were.

—My sincerest apologies.

—I forgive you the mistake because you are a foreigner.

—Can I call on you? I whispered to her.

—At midnight, she whispered back.

But the duenna had stopped and was staring at us now, so the Señorita turned her back to me and walked away.

At midnight I waited by the side door until a woman appeared, covered in a veil and holding a candle. She blew out the candle immediately and lead me into the house by a side door. I followed her up a flight of stairs and into a luxurious bedchamber. Of course it was Señorita Ignacia. She threw herself into my arms and began sobbing.

—Señor, have pity on me! I made a terrible mistake and started an affair with a drunken brute. If I don't do what he wants, he will denounce me in public as a whore!

I was stunned.

—Won't that get him in trouble, too?

—We will both end up before the Inquisition, but he doesn't care.

She pulled down the sleeve of her blouse and revealed a bruise.

—You see? I can show this to you only because you are a stranger in Madrid. Will you help me?

—But what can I do?

—Come tomorrow at the same time. Now you must go away!

I kissed her hand and descended the stairs as quietly as possible.

The next night I waited by the side door for an hour, but she did not come out. I was just about to give up and return to my lodgings in the Calle de la Cruz. Suddenly, Señorita Ignacia appeared like a madwoman in the street, her face distraught, her hair wild, her attire in disarray.

—Gracias Dios! You are here! Come quickly!

I followed her up the stairs to her chamber. On the floor, face down, lay a tall man. A fine Toledo dagger was firmly planted in beneath his left shoulder blade. The back of his white ruffled shirt was reddened by blood. The Señorita seemed paralyzed with horror. I hugged her for a moment but she pushed me away.

—Thank you, I am not hysterical, she said. Roll back the carpet, so it doesn't get bloody. You take him by that arm, and I'll take him by this one, and we'll carry him outside.

We struggled with the body to get it down the stairs and out into the street. At that hour in Madrid, everybody you see is carrying somebody else home from the tavern, so we did not arouse any suspicions. We dumped the body in an alley. I knelt down and slit open and emptied his purse so whoever discovered the body would assume that greed was the motive for this murder.

The Señorita's face was white as an eggshell. She vomited in the street. I gripped her shoulders and told her not to faint.

—It is done, I said. You are safe. No one will ever dream that a girl could kill this monster, this beast.

—How can I repay you for your help?

—I only want the gold ring from your finger to remember you by, because we must never be seen together again. I shall leave Madrid very soon.

She pulled off the ring and gave it to me without a word. Then she ran back to her house. I went to a small tavern and drank wine to calm down.

In the morning, my eyes were hardly open when someone began knocking at my door. It was one of Don Pedro's footmen. Don Pedro was waiting in a carriage for me.

—Did you get the ring?

It was sitting in my pocket. But I did not want to drag it into this game.

—No. I couldn't She is surrounded by aunts and duennas. Don Pedro smiled with faint disdain.

—Then you lost the wager and must pay. I hope this will teach you not to overestimate your abilities.

—On the contrary, it teaches me that I have been underestimating my abilities. I found out that I can think and act swiftly in an emergency. I admire myself more than ever.

Dux Castle, Bohemia, June 1791

I no longer hear the dogs. The Count must be out hunting.

The candle is almost finished, but pale light emerges in the east window, allowing me to continue writing.

I am at peace for the first time in my life.

Fishing for Smoked Salmon

Say Banana

On a fair day in early September, one of those fortunate conjunctions of summer's warmth and autumn's clarity, Martin stopped in the park on his way back to the jewelry shop. All day the brightness of the sun and the light breeze had seemed somehow remote from him. It was like being told, second-hand, that the weather was fine. He was still in a gloomy mood when he sat down on a bench. My first mistake was…he thought, then stopped. Which of his many mistakes had been the first? Leaving school? Marrying? Allowing his wife to pressure her father, a jeweler, into hiring Martin to work in his shop?

Indeed, Martin was ill-suited for a profession that demanded attention to detail and consummate social skills. At first Martin s father-in-law put him behind the sales counter, but Martin didn't know how to convince a customer to make an extravagant purchase. The women shoppers, especially, had no confidence in him. Martin's father-in-law subsequently transferred him to the workbench, so that he could learn the craft of polishing and remounting stones, but Martin spent half his time on hands and knees, searching for gems that had slipped out of his fingers.

Finally the old man demoted Martin to sweeping and delivering. He said he was giving Martin another chance, but he had already decided that his daughter's husband could do no right. He frequently pointed out clumps of dust that Martin's broom had missed. Day by day the shop seemed to get smaller and smaller until Martin felt it squeeze against his chest and restrict his breathing. No wonder he found the sight of a park bench on a beautiful day irresistible. No customers, no tension, just mothers pushing prams, children at play, old men reading newspapers. At last Martin began to relax and feel the sun. He lit a cigar that he'd been given earlier in the day as a tip. The blue smoke rose. Birds twittered all around him.

When he finally got back to the shop, the angry expression on his father-in-law's face conveyed a message as clear as his words. Martin didn't argue with his dismissal. He turned and walked away with what he hoped was a quiet dignity. He went to the nearest bus stop and sat on the bench for a long time as bus after bus went by.

When he finally got home and broke the news to his wife, she threw herself on the sofa and wept like a tropical storm. She vowed to make her father take him back, but Martin refused to even consider returning to the shop.

But what could he do instead?

He had no education or special training. He was too clumsy to be a barber, too lazy to be a farmer, and he didn't rise early enough to be a baker. His most remarkable quality was his amiable disposition. He knew a lot of people, frequently ran into acquaintances in the street, was always among the first to hear the latest gossip or local joke. His wife suggested, not for the first time, that one of these jokers might know of a job for Martin.

Sensing a familiar lecture approaching, Martin reached for his hat and coat, vaguely suggesting, on his way out the door, that he was rushing out to find employment. But it was already growing dark. He walked toward the harbor, because it was downhill rather than uphill, and eventually he found himself strolling by the waterfront's notorious row of raucous brightly-lit saloons. He entered one such establishment and called for a beer. The bar was crowded with sailors looking for love and the women who overcharged them.

Martin had barely gotten his hands on a mug when an organ grinder came in, leading a monkey on a leash. Everyone turned around. The organ grinder bowed and unhooked his pet. The monkey patrolled the room on all fours, examining the crowd with delicate nostrils and red, blinking eyes, as if checking for the presence of predators or rivals.

Meanwhile the monkey's owner set up his musical hurdy-gurdy on its stand, inserted a small roll of perforated paper into a recessed spindle, and turned the crank. As soon as the melody began, the monkey jumped up and began to do a loose-limbed, sugar-plantation dance, swinging his arms and swaying his hips. Everybody applauded with inebriated enthusiasm.

The organ grinder inserted a new roll and sang a song about the indecent recreations of a sea-captain. During this salacious ditty, the monkey swaggered back and forth like an ensign on a rolling deck, with a crisp salute now and then for an officer in the crowd. The audience nearly choked with laughter.

After a few more numbers, the monkey passed the cap. It filled up rapidly.

Meanwhile, the organ grinder made his way to the bar and by chance sat down next to Martin. Out of politeness, Martin made a few complimentary remarks about the show; to his surprise, the organ grinder immediately offered to sell him the hurdy-gurdy, and throw in the monkey for free. The monkey was an expense, the man explained. He had to be fed, washed, and occasionally de-loused with special powder. When Martin expressed surprise that the man would want to give up his very livelihood, the organ grinder replied that money wasn't everything—that he dreamed of breaking into the legitimate theater.

He cleared his throat and began to recite the opening scene of Hamlet—the appearance of the ghost on the ramparts. His declamation was ringing, dramatic, and very loud, so loud indeed that the bartender told him sharply to pack up Denmark and take it outside. The organ grinder raised his fists, but Martin quickly stepped in and suggested they leave. The organ grinder glowered at the bartender for a moment, then picked up his hurdy-gurdy, snapped a leash on his monkey, and followed Martin outside.

A light drizzle fell and the cobblestones glistened under the street lights. Martin couldn't think of anywhere to go but his own home. When they arrived there he produced a bottle of brandy for himself and the organ grinder. At the organ grinder's request, Martin mixed some brandy and water in a glass and gave it to the monkey, who clutched it with both hands and drank it like a child.

The organ grinder took a mighty swig from the bottle, stood up, and launched into Shakespeare again. "What art thou that usurp'st this time of night?" he bellowed, and at that moment Mrs. Martin appeared in the kitchen in her nightgown, her face shining with cold cream. When she saw the monkey, she shrieked and covered her bosom with both arms. The monkey was even more frightened than she was; he emitted a high-pitched squeal and scrambled under the table.

Martin half-expected the organ grinder to run away, but the man coolly doffed his cap, bowed low, and apologized so profusely for the intrusion that for once Martin's wife didn't seem to know what to say. The organ grinder commanded the monkey to come out and bow, and roll over, to stand on his head, and bow again, and to kiss Mrs. Martin's hand, but the last trick failed because she jerked her hand away when the monkey touched it.

She then turned to her husband and asked him if he intended to turn their home into a circus. When he tried to calm her, she silenced him with a threat and left the kitchen. The bedroom door slammed.

Martin and the organ grinder sighed with relief.

After finishing off the bottle of brandy, they were ready to get down to business. Martin put out the wooden cigar box that contained the household's savings. Together he and the organ grinder counted out the money in the box and haggled over a price for the organ and the monkey. As soon as they reached a bargain, Martin shook hands with the organ grinder and fell asleep in his chair. When he woke up a few hours later, he felt as if his head were twice normal size and his mouth stuffed with old cotton lint. The monkey was sleeping peacefully with his head on Martin's lap.

The hurdy-gurdy was gone. So was the cigar box.

Martin staggered to the basin and splashed some water on his face. That proved to be a mistake, because it quickened his return to consciousness. The monkey yawned and scratched himself with sensuous enjoyment. Martin put on his coat, left a hasty note of apology and farewell on the kitchen table, and jerked the animal's chain to make it come along, which it did with an eagerness that Martin found irritating. The monkey did not grasp the seriousness of the situation. He seemed to think they were going out for a stroll.

They did stroll peacefully for a minute or two, but as soon as they passed a bakery, the monkey stopped and screeched at the window. It wasn't too hard to guess that he was hungry. Martin bought him a loaf of bread, which he gobbled down with disgusting alacrity. Then he dragged Martin into the grocer's next door, where he consumed five sausages, a slab of cheese, some liverwurst, two apples, and a bunch of carrots. Martin had to persuade the suspicious grocer to extend credit, because the little change he carried in his pocket did not cover the monkey's impromptu breakfast.

People smiled at the monkey on the street, and little children pointed at him with a mixture of shyness and wonder. Martin decided that he might as well put the beast to work right away—take him to the park, put on a show, pass the hat. But when they arrived at the park, the monkey wouldn't perform. Martin tried ordering, cajoling, even mimicking the monkey's own dance style. Instead of following suit, the monkey scratched his head and walked off, the leash trailing behind him in the grass. Not knowing what else to do, Martin picked up the end of the leash and let the monkey lead. The monkey marched out of the park, down the road, and into a pub.

At this time of morning, the place was empty save for a few old men. To their amusement, the animal circled around the floor until he found a spot that seemed to make him happy. Sensing a performance about to commence, Martin unhooked the leash. The monkey did a handspring, pranced back and forth with comical arrogance, climbed on a table and snatched a hat from the hat rack and put it on his head. The men at the bar were a little bit frightened by the sight of this agile animal bouncing on the furniture, lashing his tail. But when the monkey jumped back on the floor and made a bow, there was a smattering of nervous applause from the bar, and Martin passed the hat. It was all too clear to him that the poor degraded beast did not enjoy parks and fresh air, but preferred dim lights, stale smoke, and the company of degenerates.

Just how low the animal had fallen became evident as soon as Martin tried to reattach the leash. The monkey emitted a shriek of protest, wiggled out of Martin's grasp, and scrambled onto a bar stool. Turning his back to Martin, he rapped peremptorily on the bar and held one finger up. Giggling, the barmaid drew him a beer and watched in delight as the monkey held it in both paws and gulped it down: glug glug glug. Martin swiftly hooked the leash to the collar but the monkey still resisted; he gripped the counter with both hands and bared his teeth in an ugly grimace. Martin had a sudden urge to jerk the animal off the stool, but feared that public-house opinion would go against him if he did so. The barmaid placed another beer in front of the beast, who quaffed it down like an Australian on holiday. Foam dripped from his wizened face and he grinned broadly, as if he'd just done something extremely clever. For a moment he was indistinguishable from everybody else at the bar.

Frustrated, Martin slapped some of the coins he'd just collected on the bar and ordered a pint for himself. After a couple of more draughts, the monkey suddenly hopped off the stool and made for the door. Martin followed and the two of them lurched into the full sunshine of day. They proceeded to another pub, where the monkey put on his show again, or a variation of it; he was a great improviser. Martin's hat jingled with change and he had momentary visions of prosperity. But the applause wasn't even over when the beast leaped atop the nearest barstool and began to convey the urgency of his thirst with yips and gestures. Despite Martin's insistent tugging on the leash, he drank three pints rapidly. Martin finally managed to convince the man behind the bar to stop serving him.

Back on the street, the monkey strained at his leash, eager to continue his pub crawl. Martin found it almost impossible to hold back the animal, whose willpower verged on monomania. He dragged Martin from the middle of town to the poorer neighborhoods where sooty brick bungalows lined street after street in drab reiteration. The foul air reverberated with the sounds of crashing pots and pans and the coughing of old men who had toiled all their lives in the chemical pits.

The show didn't go over very well in this part of town. The locals were more annoyed than pleased by the monkey's antics. They called Martin a drunk, a tramp, and a bad influence on an innocent creature of God. Martin protested that it was the other way round, that the monkey was a bad influence on him, but people only turned their backs to him. Later that evening in a seedy pub, the monkey attempted a double flip from the edge of a table and fell smack on his face, bloodying his nose. Rough hands seized both Martin and the animal and ejected them both into the street with practiced efficiency. A few swift kicks to their prone bodies and the ritual was complete.

Martin groaned and made an effort to sit up. His shirt was torn. It was raining again.

He set off in a random direction, more out of an impulse to flee than a desire to go anywhere in particular. Halfway down the street the monkey emitted a piercing cry, scrambled frantically, and leaped on Martin's back. Martin staggered, almost collapsing under the impact. He yelled and tried to dislodge the beast, but the monkey only held on more tightly, squeezing Martin's battered ribs and breathing heavy, fetid, beery fumes into Martin's face. Furious, Martin ran backwards and crashed the monkey into the wall of a house in an attempt to dislodge him. The creature held on tight and bit into Martin's shoulder. With a cry of pain, Martin staggered backward and the two of them collapsed into a heap of bloody fur, wet clothes, and bruised feelings. The animal went into a spasm and vomited onto the pavement beside Martin's prone body.

With the monkey still clinging to his neck, Martin struggled to his feet. Stupefied, directionless, he trudged the dark drizzling streets, empty in this dreary hour except for a few frightened alley cats. At last he descended along the embankment of the river and sought shelter under a bridge where a few moldy-smelling vagrants huddled together like abandoned piles of snoring rags. Martin sneezed a few times, then fell asleep with the monkey on top of him like a warm rug.

At the first noise of morning traffic on the bridge above, Martin woke up The monkey was lying next to him, still deep in slumber. Moving with extreme caution, hardly even daring to breath, Martin attempted to sneak away, but the monkey woke up immediately, because his leash had somehow gotten tangled around Martin's foot. Martin swore and cursed but there was nothing to be done. At least the animal didn't insist on riding Martin's back. He stayed close to Martin, loping along in a semi-upright position, laying his knuckles on the ground and swinging his body forward in easy rhythm. Martin tried to pretend he wasn't there, but he knew the animal was following him. It especially galled him to see the delighted faces of people in the street, charmed by the sight of this depraved and selfish brute.

Every time he passed a greengrocer's the monkey snatched an apple or a plum from the stall, making Martin tremble with fear of arrest. He thought about beating up the monkey, but feared that the monkey might fight back—the animal had grown up the jungle and probably knocked around in a lot of tough seaports.

No, the situation called for finesse.

Martin stuck his hands in his pockets and began to whistle as if he hadn't a care in the world. Strolling along with a great show of insouciance, he led his unsuspecting companion to the main entrance of the National Zoological Gardens. Their appearance caused a stir of excitement among the children and their mothers and nannies who were queued up at the gate. Martin and the monkey marched straight in as if they had business at the zoo; the man at the door didn't even ask them for tickets. Once inside, the monkey began to behave erratically, shrieking at the birds, gibbering at the hippos, and leaping in fear on Martin's back when they passed the lions.

When they got to the monkey cage, Martin's monkey hopped over the iron fence, climbed halfway up the bars and began to squeal wildly, provoking an uproar among the simians inside. Several uniformed keepers appeared and seized Martin's monkey. They pried his fingers off the bars and wrestled him to the ground. Martin tried to slip away in the confusion but a policeman ordered him to remain where he was. The Assistant Director of Primates arrived a moment later and examined Martin's monkey carefully, looking at his fur, his eyes, his ears. When he attempted to open the monkey's lips to examine his teeth, the monkey deftly opened the Assistant Director's lips and peered back at him.

By this time a crowd had gathered, and they roared.

Flushed with embarrassment, the Assistant Director declared Martin's monkey a shabby specimen fit only for a provincial circus, and ordered Martin to remove it from the zoo's premises forthwith. The policeman jerked his thumb in the direction of the exit. Cursing his bad luck, Martin hurried away, dragging the monkey behind him.

He didn't notice that a man was following him, a well-dressed man, with a neat gray beard and an expensive umbrella under his arm. As soon as Martin and the monkey were outside the gate, the gray-bearded man accosted them, saying that he had just witnessed the scene inside the zoo and was deeply impressed with the monkey's wit. He expressed surprise that the zoo had refused to accept such an evidently talented creature.

Martin was in no mood to stand around and listen to a stranger compliment his monkey, so he told the man to come to the point. The man explained that he was a doctor of animal psychology, and he wanted to use the monkey in a philosophical inquiry he was conducting. It was all completely harmless; no drugs or surgery would be involved. Furthermore, he was prepared to remunerate Martin for the privilege of working with his remarkable beast.

For a moment Martin's whole world turned upside down and he had to secretly pinch himself to make sure he wasn't simply hallucinating this offer. Somebody was willing to buy his monkey? Feigning nonchalance, Martin said it would great inconvenience to be separated from the monkey, not to mention an agony of loneliness, but perhaps he would consider making a sacrifice for the great cause of scientific investigation. The doctor suggested that Martin accompany him to his laboratory.

They went by cab to a fashionable neighborhood, mounted the stairs of an imposing house, and were greeted at the door by a real butler. He lead them along a corridor and down a flight of stairs, where they were greeted by a cacophony of barks, meows, squeaks, squawks, and hoots. There was a real menagerie in the cellar, and most of the animals roamed loose: the cats and dogs, the mynah birds and parrots perched on wooden hat-racks, the piglets and gerbils nesting in boxes full of straw. Several white-coated lab assistants were helping an old woman scoop turds into a burlap bag. A heavy stench pervaded the room, and probably always would.

The doctor explained that his research had lead him from the more orthodox areas of biology into zoolinguistics and the possibility of communication between homo sapiens and other species. He decided that the first step was to teach an animal to speak; after various experiments, he decided to try using a primate. He had been looking for likely candidates for some time, trying to establish some standard of simian intelligence, but all that seemed a waste of time now in light of the amazing facility for responsiveness that Martin's monkey had demonstrated at the zoo.

Martin said he was impressed by the doctor's dedication to science, and was particularly interested to know how much he was willing to invest in the future of his investigations, more specifically, how much he was willing to pay for the monkey. The doctor shrugged and asked Martin how much he wanted. Martin named a sum that was substantial enough to mollify Mrs. Martin and restore domestic harmony, at least for a while. The doctor thought for a moment, and asked Martin if he had ever seen a Grand Palabra Island parrot before. He pointed out a great bird with green, yellow and orange-red feathers. It was sitting on a swing in an open cage. When it heard the doctor's voice, the bird whistled a greeting, flew out of the cage, and alighted on the doctor's outstretched hand. The doctor passed the parrot to Martin's hand. It climbed up to Martin's shoulder and gave him a peck on the cheek with his beak, not exactly a kiss but close enough.

According to the doctor, this rare and valuable parrot possessed a vocabulary of several hundred words, not just a random collection of utterances, either, but real responses that it knew when and how to use. It could ask for food, it sang "Happy Birthday" at parties, it congratulated you sarcastically when you dropped and broke something, and so forth. Moreover, it had the capacity to learn a lot more words. But it was currently doing nothing and serving no purpose. The doctor had recently finished all his experiments with the parrot, and now he didn't know what to do with it. Maybe he could find somebody who wanted to make a lot of money from exhibiting it to the public. Unfortunately, at the moment the doctor didn't know anybody like that.

Martin asked if the bird drank.

The doctor said that the bird needed fresh water every day.

And that's how Martin ended up with a Grand Palabra parrot. As he carried the cage up the stairs, the monkey started to follow but two lab assistants grabbed the beast and pushed him into a cage, the only cage in the whole menagerie. The monkey shrieked, howled, bared his teeth, and pounded on the wire mesh. He scared the cats and dogs and made the birds flutter away to the other end of the basement—but all to no avail.

Martin was gone.

The monkey was quiet for a minute. Then he beat on the wire mesh screen again. In response a lab assistant banged on the side of the cage and told him to shut up. All the dogs barked in a collective canine frenzy, and for a fleeing moment the monkey was glad to be separated from them by steel wire, although he would have much preferred to have the dogs inside and himself out. He looked around at his new accommodations, which were remarkably Spartan. There was a cup of water in the cage, he noticed, but his chances of getting a pint of ale served to him were probably very slim. Lacking any better diversion, he curled up and went to sleep.

In the morning when he woke up, there was no food in the cage. It didn't bother him; he'd been hungry before. None of his former owners had been good or steady providers. He was used to that. But the cage! The cage bothered him. For the first time in years he yearned to reach for branches and swing from tree to tree.

Presently the doctor appeared with a banana. It was spotted, overripe and delicious. The monkey got excited and began to chatter. The lab assistants crowded around the cage and stared at him, making him recoil; the sight of so many eager, smooth, and ugly faces was profoundly disconcerting. Then the doctor came forward. He brought the banana closer and began to repeat the same two sounds over and over again: one sound, then another sound uttered twice. A rhythm, a cadence, accompanied by the waggling of the yellow fruit.

Together, the three sounds made a word.

Now the monkey had spent most of his life in human society and was familiar with the phenomenon of human speech. He'd passed through the hands of many feckless masters, men who spoke to him in the dark of night as if he were a child, a confessor, even an intimate companion. But he never bothered to listen carefully to any of the babbling. He had danced for his dinner and clowned for his supper, but he had never mimicked the ugly sounds that humans inflict on each other. Even now, hungry as he was, he resisted; he turned his back and covered his head with his arms.

When they returned that afternoon, he was famished, but still stubborn. The doctor chanted, the banana dangled, the monkey rolled over on his side and remained silent.

Next morning, the doctor and his assistants held out the ripe yellow fruit again, and again they repeated the syllables. Surely they would give up, thought the monkey. Surely they would not let him die of starvation! But after an hour or so of taking turns with the banana, they looked at their watches and shrugged. The doctor actually put the banana in the pocket of his lab coat. As he walked away, the monkey panicked.

"Banana," he croaked.

They all stopped and turned around in amazement. Blinking with surprise, the doctor approached, brandishing the banana in front of the cage door.

"Banana," said the monkey again.

The doctor opened a slot in the cage door and shoved the banana in. The monkey ate it greedily. By this time all the assistants were yelling and slapping each other on the back. They opened a bottle of champagne and ended up slopping more of it on their coats than in their fine crystal glasses. The monkey desperately wanted some champagne, but he didn't know the word for it. He could only manage a distant approximation. "Ale," he said. "Ale!" But nobody heard him. They were too busy shouting and congratulating each other.

The next morning they brought him several bananas and made him say the word each time he wanted one. That was humiliating enough, but there was more to come. When he became thirsty, he discovered there was nothing to drink in his cage. The doctor held the cup in front of the cage door and repeated the sounds that he wanted the monkey to make.

The monkey knew he was defeated. "Water," he said.

The doctor immediately opened the cage door and gave him the cup of water. As he drank it down, the lab assistants applauded. The monkey resented this. He decided to speak as little as possible. If they wanted him to perform, they should make him comfortable and serve him pints instead of caging him up and withholding his food.

The next day the doctor came in with a carrot and repeated its name. But every time he heard the word "carrot," the monkey said "banana." The lab assistants discreetly drifted away, one by one, until the doctor and the monkey were left alone together, locked in a mutual fury of exasperation, each repeating his word with emphasis, carrot, banana, back and forth, until the doctor finally lost his temper and uttered an obscenity. Instantly the monkey repeated the expletive he had heard so often from sailors: "Fuck you!"

The doctor was flabbergasted. For some reason, he thrust the carrot inside the cage and strode off with an angry look on his face.

The monkey sighed with relief. He sat down in the cage with his knees up and his arms around his legs. Time went by, and he began to feel bored and restless. Just when he was ready to scream, another face loomed behind the cage door. It was old, wrinkled, benevolent. After a moment, the monkey recognized it as the old lady who came downstairs once or twice a day to help the lab assistants clean up. She tapped on the cage with her forefinger and made little clucking noises, just as she might use to attract the attention of a kitten or a puppy.

"Ale," croaked the monkey.

But it was the wrong word to say. The old lady seemed horrified. She made a rapid motion with her hand over her bosom, the same gesture the monkey had seen among sailors in the Mediterranean during a violent squall. The old lady hurried away muttering to herself.

All was quiet for hours. Then, sometime during the night, the monkey heard the basement door creak open, followed by light footsteps descending the stairs. It was the old lady. She made her way past the dozing animals, taking the utmost care not to disturb them. A few cats followed her, but otherwise peace prevailed.

The old lady drew up a chair in front of the monkey's cage, pulled a black book from her pocket, and began reading to him aloud in a soft but passionate vibrato. Her eyes occasionally flickered up to look in his. Her merest glance seemed to burn in the darkness

The first surprise was that he could understand human speech. In fact he had always understood it, but he had never known that he knew it until now. It was only the urgency and conviction in the old lady's voice that shocked him into such a realization. Maybe the doctor's promptings had something to do with it as well.

The second surprise was what he understood. First there was darkness, then a really big ape named God created light, and then God separated light from darkness. Why? Right here in this dim basement, dark and light were all mixed up. Would it look better if all the light was on one side and all the darkness on the other? The story of creation seemed senseless to him. However, he was deeply affected by the expulsion from the Garden. He thought of his carefree youth in the forest where bananas grow wild and began to snivel with grief. The old lady put her finger to her lips and shushed him, telling him gently to go to sleep. She closed the black book and went back upstairs.

All night the words of human speech overflowed the monkey's thoughts, awakening memories, giving them new meanings. He barely slept a wink. In the morning the doctor tapped on the cage door, but the exhausted monkey merely yawned and farted. Annoyed, the doctor hammered against the side of the cage with his fist. Reluctantly, the monkey woke up, stretched, and scratched himself. The doctor held an apple out in front of cage door and repeated the word loudly.

"Banana," said the monkey.

The doctor repeated the word for apple, and suddenly the monkey remembered the story that the old lady had read to him the night before; his mind jumped from apple to Eden to an old memory of being dragged aboard ship in a net. He gibbered and shrieked at the doctor, uttered gross insults that would be dangerous to hurl at another monkey. The doctor did not understand them, of course, but he darkly sensed that the monkey was getting personal with him. He ordered his lab assistants to withhold all food and water for twenty-four hours. The monkey was enraged, but all he could really do was show his teeth. That made some birds squawk, and a stocky bulldog barked aggressively.

Late that evening the old lady crept downstairs with her black book again.

She sat down and began to read a story about somebody named Noah who became intoxicated and lay uncovered in his tent. It sounded like good fun to the monkey, but the old lady seemed to disapprove of Noah's behavior. Feeling ashamed of himself, the monkey retreated to the back of his cage and furiously slapped himself on the head with both hands as punishment for his own sins.

However, he had to stop almost immediately. The very act of hurting himself was so un-animal-like that he simply couldn't manage to do it.

The old lady smiled. She skipped ahead to a story called Exodus. It was difficult to understand, but the monkey enjoyed being read to. Every time the old lady became tired and her voice trailed off, he squealed loudly to wake her up. Eventually she could continue no more; she closed the book with a yawn. But the monkey was in fever of excitement. Without even thinking, he spoke up.

"Let me go," he said.

The old lady went rigid. Her mouth opened once or twice but no sound came up.

"I command thee, open this cage now!"

She undid the latch with quivering fingers. The monkey hopped out of the cage. Immediately the other animals in the basement began barking and meowing and twittering. The monkey snarled at them and made for the stairs, but when he got to the top, he fumbled around with the doorknob. It'd always given him trouble. The old lady mounted the stairs and opened the door for him, then took him by the arm and lead him down the main corridor of the house, which was dark except for a few glowing sconces. She opened the front door and stood there as if she didn't know whether to go or stay.

"Remember this day, that I came out of Egypt," said the monkey. She fainted.

Feeling the urgent need to put as much space between him and the doctor's house as possible, the monkey began to lope down the street rapidly. It was just dawn. The cool morning air, the sound of birds in the municipal trees, even the sight of brick and pavement lifted his spirits. The few people who were going to work early were startled to see him alone and at large. The monkey hurried around the corner and ran straight into a bus stop crowded with laborers. They began to hoot and shout and laugh when they saw him. One man pulled a ham sandwich from his lunch box and approached the monkey, waving it like a matador waves his cape. The monkey avoided him and shimmied up the pole of a street lamp. When he got to the top, he spread his arms and began to orate. His voice was rough and rasping, and speaking made his throat raw, but he felt an urgency to express himself.

"People! Among the multitudes of animals, I have been given the power of the word! I have gone from darkness unto light, from confinement to freedom, from silence to speech. I have gone from ale to stout, from stout to beer, and from beer to nothing, just water. Now I am come amongst you to deliver a message. People, my message is, that animals should be free! Whoever puts a creature in a cage, especially a monkey, is worse than Pharaoh of Egypt. The sacred covenant between God and gorilla must never be broken! Let my creatures go!"

A hubbub ensued at the bus stop. Everybody had a different idea of what the monkey had said. Some people thought that the monkey's speech was a prearranged stunt designed to make fun of either the theory of evolution or the Bible. Fistfights broke out. The monkey dangled from the top of the street light and tried to make himself heard one more time: "I say unto you, we must free all the animals! The Lord has commanded me to lead you to the zoo and break open all the cages of all creatures who walk upon the earth, except the lions!"

Before anybody could react to this stirring call to action, the doctor came around the corner followed by servants and family members, all of them in disarray, wearing coats thrown over pajamas, their unkempt hair waving and slippers flapping. When the doctor saw the monkey on top of the street light, he announced that the monkey belonged to him and that he would give a large sum to have it back.

Alarmed, the monkey cried, "Pay no heed to that man! No man or beast belongs to any another! The Lord has given me the power of speech to tell you this message!"

The crowd fell silent, and for half a second the monkey thought he had convinced them. But a disgruntled voice in the back piped up to say that monkeys can't talk, that everybody knows monkeys can't talk, so why were they all listening to this fraud, this impostor, this false prophet?

The doctor took advantage of the moment of doubt; he doubled his reward.

Burly men charged forward and shoved each other out of the way in their haste to climb the lamppost and capture the fugitive. The monkey balanced himself, then leaped from the top of the street light to the nearest roof. The excitement in the street was wild.

After traveling from roof to roof, now and then startling a housewife who was shaking out her mop, the monkey came to the last in a row of adjacent buildings. All he could do was go down a drainpipe. He frantically looked around for low wall or a leafy bush to hide under, but saw nothing better than a discarded newspaper on a stone bench. Imitating a familiar yet mysterious human behavior, he sat on the bench and held the newspaper outstretched in front of him, so that it covered all but his fingers

Two men came running down the street. To his consternation, they stopped and began to make comments about the roof of the nearby building and possible means of access to it. The monkey froze. He wanted to flee, but instead, he said, "Did they catch that crazy monkey yet?"

One of the men expressed surprise that the story was already in the newspaper. Then they both set off in hot pursuit once more. As soon as the street was empty for a moment, the monkey put down his paper and hurried into a courtyard. Discovering some trash bins there, he crawled inside the least evil-smelling one and crouched inside it until late at night. When the world outside was perfectly quiet, he went out in the street and made his way toward the harbor, finding his way through the dark streets by following the scent of the sea. Whenever he saw somebody coming, he hid in the shadows. At last he reached the docks. He swung himself up the mooring rope of a large ocean-going vessel and stowed away in the hold. And though he spent many years at sea, and heard many aggravating remarks, and was often misunderstood, he never spoke another word.

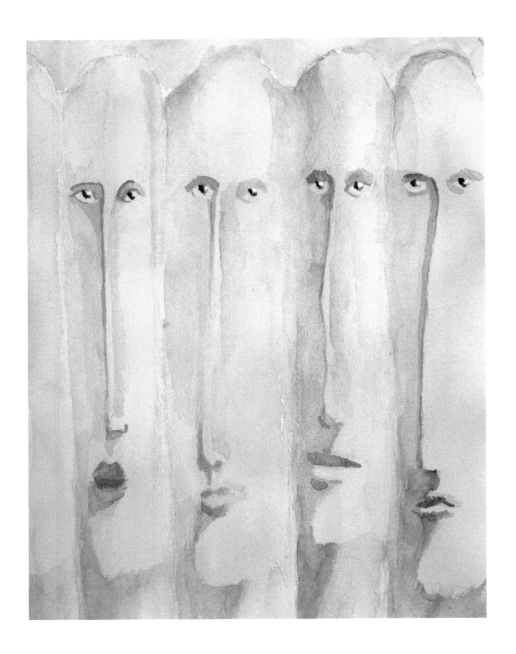